ICONIC FIGURES

volume 2

ICONIC FIGURES

volume 2

MOONSTONE

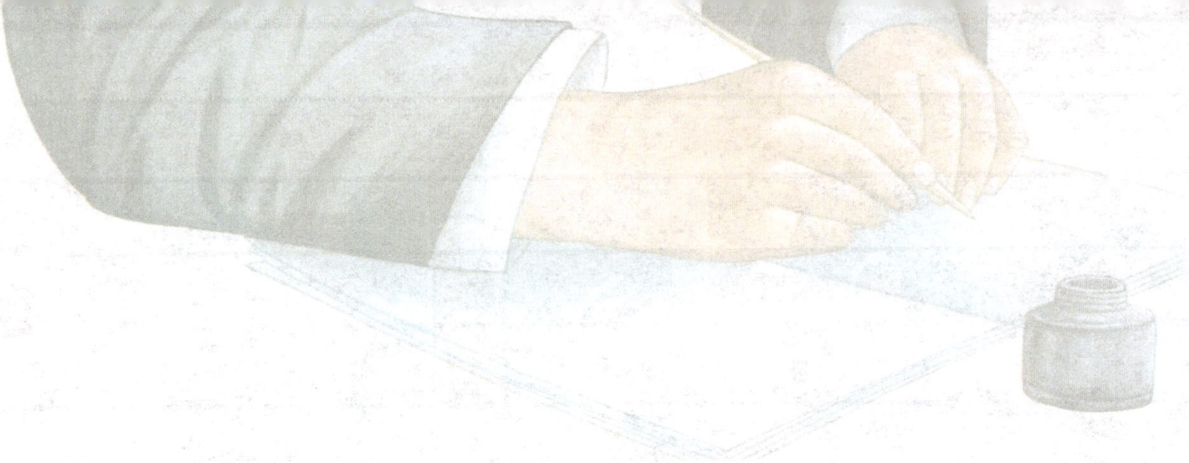

Published in Moonstone
by Rupa Publications India Pvt. Ltd 2023
7/16, Ansari Road, Daryaganj
New Delhi 110002

Sales centres:
Prayagraj Bengaluru Chennai
Hyderabad Jaipur Kathmandu
Kolkata Mumbai

P-ISBN: 978-93-5702-332-0
E-ISBN: 978-93-5702-330-6

First impression 2023

10 9 8 7 6 5 4 3 2 1

Printed in India

Contents

Great Authors

Great Painters

Great Musicians

Great Scientists

Great Authors

Introduction

The only profession that permits us to shape our universe is writing. Who would believe that this delightful world had been created with a pen's tiny nib? Numerous well-known authors have successfully imagined and painted this world in vivid detail. Owning their creativity, they rose to fame and attained a prominent position in society. Authors like Shakespeare, Charles Dickens, Jane Austen and many others changed the way we perceive this creation. Today, we read their works for a variety of reasons, including knowledge and the pursuit of happiness that reading brings.

William Shakespeare

William Shakespeare is the first name that strikes our minds when we think of English literature. He was regarded as the greatest writer in the English language owing to his fame as a playwright. His writings did, however, extend beyond the framework of drama and into the realm of poetry, gaining him the title 'England's national poet'.

Early Childhood and Education

Shakespeare was born in the town of Stratford-upon-Avon. He is believed to have been born on April 23, 1564. Shakespeare's father, John Shakespeare, was a tanner of leathers and an apprentice glover, and his mother, Mary Arden, was from a wealthy landowning farmer's family. He attended Stratford Grammar School.

INTERESTING FACT

Shakespeare vanished from history after the birth of his twins. For those seven years, there is no record of his whereabouts. This period in Shakespeare's life is known as his 'Lost Years.'

Marriage

He married when he was only 18 years old. Anne Hathaway, his pregnant wife, was 26 years old. They tied the knot on November 28, 1582, and on May 26, 1583, Anne gave birth to a little girl. Shakespeare and Anne later had twin children on February 3, 1585.

Work

Shakespeare is thought to have begun writing between 1590 and 1613. He was in London by 1592 and made a name for himself as an actor and playwright. He is well-known for his plays *Romeo and Juliet, King John, Richard II,* and *Love's Labour's Lost.* His works include over 38 plays, 154 sonnets, and several poems.

Death

Shakespeare breathed his last on 23 April, 1616. He was buried in the chancel of the Holy Trinity Church.

Charles Dickens

Charles John Huffam Dickens, a prolific English novelist, was considered as the greatest author of the Victorian Period. Many regard him as a spokesman for the underclass, as his work depicts the miserable lives of the poor and oppressed.

Early Life

Charles Dickens was born on February 7, 1812, in Landport, Hampshire. His father, John Dickens, worked as a clerk in the Navy pay office, and his extravagant lifestyle frequently caused financial difficulties. Dickens' love of books began in his childhood when he discovered his little world through the readings of *Robinson Crusoe, Arabian Nights, Don Quixote,* and *Tom Jones.*

INTERESTING FACT

Dickens' wife Catherine was the daughter of the editor of the Evening Chronicle, where Dickens worked as a journalist.

His Career and Work

He worked as a reporter for newspapers and the Parliament. Dickens started penning short tales and essays for periodicals in 1833. *Pickwick Papers,* a collection of comic narratives that served as his debut novel, was released in 1836. He published numerous autobiographies, novels, and travel books, produced weekly periodicals, and oversaw non-profit organisations. Dickens also performed a play for Queen Victoria in 1851.

His later life

Dickens moved to Gadshill Place, near Rochester, Kent, after divorcing his wife Catherine in 1958. He delivered lectures in Britain and the United States for the next ten years. During one of his lectures in England, he suffered a stroke, and the very next day, on June 9, 1870, he passed away at his home in Kent. On June 14, his body was laid to rest in Westminster Abbey's poets' corner.

Jane Austen

Jane Austen was one of the major English novelists of the nineteenth century. Her writing is renowned for its strong narratives and elegant compositions. *Pride and Prejudice, Sense and Sensibility,* and *Northanger Abbey* are a few of her best-known works.

Early Life and Education

Jane Austen was born on December 16, 1775, at the rectory in the Hampshire village of Steventon. Cassandra, her only sister, was her constant companion. She received her early education from her father. She and her sister Cassandra later attended a boarding school to receive formal education. However, due to financial constraints, they returned home and completed their education under the supervision of their father.

INTERESTING FACT

Austen wrote her first novel when she was fourteen years old. She named it 'Love and Friendship' even though she couldn't spell friendship correctly.

Her Work

Austen had been exposed to drama and comedy since she was a child. Her siblings would frequently stage plays at home. Austen wrote many poems, comic pieces and stories for her family's recreation in her early adolescence. Her writings between 1787 and 1793 were later compiled and became known as *Austen's Juvenalia.* Around 1795, Austen began work on her famous novel *Pride and Prejudice,* which she initially titled *First Impression.* At the same time, she began work on another one of her famous works, *Northanger Abbey.*

Later Life

Jane continued to write, and during this time, she revised *Sense and Sensibility* and had it published anonymously. It was followed by two more extremely popular works, *Emma* and *Mansfield Park.* She started her best work, *Persuasion,* in August 1815 and finished it in 1816.

Last Days

Austen's health began to deteriorate from 1816 onwards. In May 1817, she was transferred to Winchester for treatment, where she died on July 18, 1817, at the age of 41.

Fyodor Dostoevsky

Fyodor Mikhailovich Dostoevsky was a well-known Russian author. He is best known for his novels Crime and Punishment and The Brothers Karamazov, and his works include novels, short stories, and essays.

Early childhood and Education

Dostoevsky was born on November 11, 1821, in Moscow. His father was a retired army physician. Initially, Dostoevsky was home-schooled and after his education in Moscow, he enrolled in the Army Engineering College in St. Petersburg. In 1837, Dostoevsky's mother died, and his woes were exacerbated when his father died in 1839, leaving him an orphan.

Work

In 1846, he published his first novel, *Poor Folk*. Following that, *The Double*, another of his brilliant works, was published. Dostoevsky joined a socialist group in 1846 and was arrested in 1849. He was imprisoned in Siberia for four years and his time there inspired many of his works like *Winter Notes on Summer Impressions*, *The Insulted and Injured*, and *The House of the Dead*.

INTERESTING FACT

Dostoevsky was 46 years old at the time of his second marriage. His wife, on the other hand, was only 22 years old.

Marriage and later life

In 1857, he married Maria Isaeva, a 29-year-old widow. Dostoevsky worked as an editor of the monthly periodical from 1861 to 1863. He married Anna Snitkina, a stenographer, in 1867. Dostoevsky's health deteriorated in 1880, and he died on February 9, 1881.

Maxim Gorky

Maxim Gorky, the greatest Russian literary figure of the twentieth century, was a Russian short story writer, novelist, autobiographer, and essayist. Better known as the 'Father of Revolutionary Literature,' his works reflect the cultural and political activities of his generation.

Early life

Maxim Gorky, was born on March 16, 1868, in the city of Nizhny Novgorod. Gorky's father died when he was only four years old. Gorky received only a few months of formal education due to financial constraints. Gorky did a variety of odd jobs as a child including a dishwasher, an assistant in a shoemaker's shop and a worker for an icon painter.

INTERESTING FACT

Gorky's original name was Alexei Maximovich Peshkov. He named himself Gorky, which means bitter, due to the bitterness of his early life experiences.

His work

Gorky began his career as a journalist for a provincial newspaper. *Essays and Stories,* his first book, was published in 1898. Gorky's first novel, *Foma Gordeyev,* was published in 1899, and he went on to write many more. Gorky's works reflect his rage at society's discrimination against poor people. He also wrote plays, the most well-known of which was The *Lower Depths.* In 1914, he published his first biographical novel, *My Childhood,* followed by *In the World* in 1916.

His later life

Gorky had pneumonia and experienced its effects from time to time. He died on June 18, 1936. His ashes were interred at the Kremlin Wall in Moscow, Russian Federation.

Rabindranath Tagore

Rabindranath Tagore was a prolific writer, a great poet, philosopher, music composer and painter. He spread the knowledge of Indian culture around the world through his writings. He won the Nobel Prize in Literature for his collection of famous poems *Gitanjali* and became Asia's first Nobel Laureate.

Early Childhood and Education

Tagore was born in Calcutta on May 7, 1861. He was the youngest of fourteen siblings. Maharishi Debendranath Tagore, his father, was a wealthy Sanskrit scholar. Tagore wrote his first poem when he was eight years old. He liked reading about astronomy, history, Kalidasa's classical poetry, modern science, and biographies. Tagore went to England at the age of seventeen to become a lawyer. However, he was unable to complete his degree and returned home in 1880.

INTERESTING FACT

Tagore received a knighthood from the British Crown in 1915. However, he rejected it in 1919 because of the Jallianwala Bagh Massacre.

Work and Marriage

Tagore's first collection of poems was published when he was seventeen years old. Tagore married Mrinalini, a ten-year-old girl, in 1883. Tagore published some of his works between 1891 and 1895, the most admired of which was *Galpaguchchha*, a collection of 84 stories. Manasi, *Gitanjali*, and *Gitimalya* are among his most important works.

Later life

In 1937, Tagore fell ill and never fully recovered. Despite his illness, he created some of his finest works in the last five years of his life. Rabindranath Tagore died on August 7, 1941, at the family estate Jorasanko.

Mark Twain

Mark Twain was an American writer, journalist and humorist. He ranked among the great literary figures of American literature. His famous works include *The Adventures of Tom Sawyer* and *Huckleberry Finn.*

INTERESTING FACT

He went by the pen name Mark Twain his entire life, but his real name was Samuel Langhorne Clemens.

Childhood

Mark Twain was born in Florida, Missouri on November 30, 1835. Twain was mischievous as a child, began smoking when he was nine years old and despised going to school. He lost his father when he was only 11 years old. He was expelled from school when he was 12 years old, and he soon began working. Twain educated himself in public libraries.

His Death

Twain spent the last years of his life working on his official autobiography. He died of a heart attack on April 21, 1910.

Twain as an Author

In 1869, Twain produced his first book of travel letters *Innocents Abroad* but the book did not bring him much fame. His book *The Gilded Age,* published in 1873, proved to be a turning point in his life. The publication of The *Adventures of Tom Sawyer, The Prince and the Pauper,* and *The Adventures of Huckleberry Finn* boosted his career. Twain was regarded as the greatest character writer in the literary community after the success of *The Adventures of Huckleberry Finn.*

Early Works

Twain began his career as an apprentice printer. In 1851, he began working for his brother Orion's newspaper, the Hannibal Journal. After working as an editor, journalist, and humorist, he decided to become a pilot. Due to the Civil War, his career as a pilot ended in 1861, and he returned to being a journalist.

Leo Tolstoy

Count Lev Nikolayevich Tolstoy, a Russian novelist, is regarded as one of the greatest of all time. His works include more than fifteen books, the most well-known of which are *The Cossacks*, *War and Peace*, and *Anna Karenina*.

Early Life

Leo Tolstoy was born in Russia on September 9, 1828, into a noble family. His father passed away when Tolstoy was nine years old, leaving him and his three siblings under the care of their family members. He was sent to the University of Kazan in 1844 to pursue a dual degree in law and languages. Tolstoy, however, left his studies in the middle and eventually went back to his estate.

Work

Tolstoy had started writing his autobiographies called *Childhood, Boyhood, and Youth*. Tolstoy left the military in 1856 to focus on his estate, Yasnaya Polyana. During this time, he wrote his masterpieces *War and Peace, The Cossacks*, and *Anna Karenina*. Over the course of the next 40 years, he wrote some of his best works like *A Short Exposition of the Gospels, What I Believe In, What Then Must We Do?* and *The Law of Love and the Law of Violence*.

INTERESTING FACT

Leo Tolstoy learned to ride a bicycle in his late sixties.

Death

Tolstoy died of pneumonia while on a pilgrimage on November 10, 1910.

Aesop

Aesop, famous for his fables, is often known as the father of fable-telling. He is believed to have written over 600 fables. His fables have become popular teaching tools for moral lessons. Aesop's fables are still used in many contemporary stories, plays and movies.

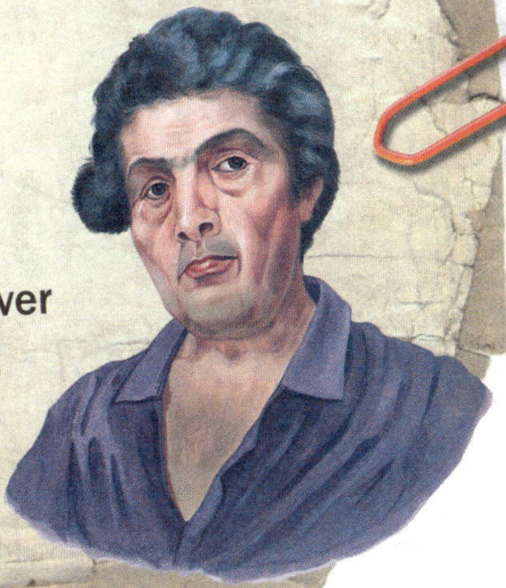

Life

His life is mostly unrecorded, but it is thought that he was born in the Southeast European country of France around 620 BCE. Aesop was cited in writings by the great philosopher Aristotle who mentioned the former being a slave first to a man named Xanthus and then to another man named Ladmon.

INTERESTING FACT

When Aesop was killed, he said, "You may kill me, but my unjust death will bring you great misfortune," and the Delphians are said to have suffered a great deal.

Work

Aesop was renowned among his teachers for having a brilliant mind. After being set free by his masters, he travelled the country giving stirring speeches and narrating his fables. Aesop is credited with creating some of the most well-known fables in history, including *The Tortoise and the Hare*, *The Ant and the Grasshopper*, *The Ant and the Dove*, *The Fox and the Goat*, and *The Thief and the Coat*. He also spent part of his life at King Croesus of Lydia's court.

Death

Aesop is thought to have died during one of his missions to Delphi. He insulted the Delphians during his mission and was accused of sacrilege, followed by his execution.

Grimm Brothers

The Grimm Brothers, Jacob Carl Grimm and Wilhelm Carl Grimm were German scholars. They are well-known for their collections of folktales and fairy tales. The Grimm Brothers are famous for compiling a German dictionary in addition to being one of the best storytellers.

Early Life and Education

The eldest of the two, Jacob Grimm, was born on January 4, 1785, and Wilhelm Grimm, the younger brother, was born on February 24, 1786, in Hanau, Germany. Philipp Grimm, their father, was a lawyer who worked as the town clerk in Hanau. They first attended Friedrichsgymnasium in Kassel, Germany, before going on to study law at the University of Marburg.

Work

Jacob began working as a librarian in the court of the King of Westphalia in Germany in 1808. In 1812, the brothers published their first collection of authentic German fairy tales. It was named *Kinder- und Hausmärchen* or *Children's and Household Tales.* They later published their second volume of folktales in 1814. *Sleeping Beauty, The Frog Prince, Hansel and Gretel, Rapunzel, Cinderella, Rumpelstiltskin,* and *Snow White* are just a few of their well-known stories.

INTERESTING FACT

The Brothers worked to explain how words from related languages—like English apple and German Apfel—are related. They created 'Grimm's law', which served as the guidelines for defining these kinds of relationships.

Later life

The first volume of their German dictionary, *Deutsches Wörterbuch,* was published in 1854. However, the Grimm Brothers didn't live long enough to see the publication of their dictionary's final version. Jacob Grimm passed away on September 20, 1863, and Wilhelm Grimm left this world on December 16, 1859.

Hans Christian Andersen

Best known for his fairy tales, Hans Christian Andersen was a Danish author and poet that emerged from the lower strata of society. He was a novelist, dramatist, and poet. His fairy tales are his finest contribution to world literature.

Early life

Hans Christian Andersen was born in Odense, Denmark on April 2, 1805. When he was seventeen, he attended Copenhagen University on a government-arranged scholarship. Andersen began writing poems, plays and stories in 1827. *The Dying Child* was his first poem. In 1828, he published his first successful narrative, which marked the start of his writing career.

Death

In 1872, Hans was deeply injured falling off from his bed. He never recovered completely after that. He breathed his last on August 4, 1875. His body was buried in the Assistens Kirkegard , Copenhagen.

INTERESTING FACT

Jenny Lind, the opera singer, held the most special place in his life, and it was in her context that Hans used the expression "Swedish Nightingale" in one of his most famous stories, "The Nightingale."

Work

His first book of fairy tales, *Eventyr,* fortalte for børn, was published in 1835. *The Tinderbox, Little Claus and Big Claus, The Princess and the Pea,* and *Little Ida's Flowers* were all popular stories in the book. Hans continued to write stories and published many volumes year after year until 1872. Hans wrote over 150 fairy tales during his lifetime, and his stories have also been translated into over 100 languages.

Lewis Carroll

Charles Lutwidge Dodgson, better known as Lewis Carroll, was an English author, logician, mathematician, and photographer. His most famous works are *Alice's Adventures in Wonderland* and its sequel, *Through the Looking-Glass.*

Early Life

Carroll was born on January 27, 1832, as the oldest child of Charles Dodgson and Frances Jane Lutwidge. He had three brothers and seven sisters. He was born in Daresbury, Cheshire. Carroll first studied at Yorkshire's Richmond School, a small private institution but he soon left and transferred to Rugby School. After finishing his studies in Rugby, he entered Christ Church in Oxford. He received honours in Mathematics in 1952, and as a result, he was soon nominated for a studentship. Later, he also pursued classics, and in 1857, he received his M.A.

INTERESTING FACT

Dodgson had a neurological condition that led to bizarre fantasies, which was given the name "Alice in Wonderland Syndrome" after his work.

Work

Carroll met the Dean of Christ Church's 4-year-old daughter, Alice Liddell, in 1856. He wrote stories for Alice and her sisters regularly over time. His humorous stories were well-liked by kids, which encouraged him to write the fantastical book *Alice's Adventures in Wonderland*. Due to the enormous popularity of this book, a sequel, *Through the Looking-Glass and What Alice Found There,* was published in 1871. Other notable Carroll works include the humorous play *Euclid and His Modern Rivals,* the epic "nonsense" poem *Hunting of the Shark,* the collection of poems *Phantasmagoria,* and the short story *Jabberwocky.*

Later Life and Death

He was writing *Sylvie and Bruno,* a two-volume novel, in the final years of his life. The book was released in 1889 and 1893. He passed away on January 14, 1898, from pneumonia, and was buried at the Mount Cemetery in Guildford.

Sir Arthur Doyle

Sir Arthur Conan Doyle was a Scottish doctor and writer. He is best known for creating the fictional character, Sherlock Holmes. Apart from detective stories, Sir Arthur contributed to a variety of literary genres including science fiction, plays, historical novels, romances and non-fiction stories.

Early Life and Education

Arthur, born on May 22, 1859, in Edinburg, Scotland. Arthur was born into a poor Irish Catholic family. Arthur graduated in 1874 and enrolled in Edinburgh University to study medicine. He worked as an assistant to Doctor Joseph Bell there. Arthur received his Master's degree in Biology in 1881 and his M.D. in 1885.

INTERESTING FACT

Sherlock Holmes' character was inspired by Dr Joseph Bell, who was Conan Doyle's medical school mentor.

Work

The Captain of the Pole-Star, The Five Orange Pips, The Heiress of Glenmahowley, J. Habakuk Jephson's Statement, and *The Man from Archangel* were among his works. Later, in 1887, he introduced his famous character Sherlock Holmes in his third novel, *A Study in Scarlet. A Scandal in Bohemia,* the first of the Sherlock Holmes detective stories, was published in 1891.

Later Life

Tired of writing about his character, Sherlock Holmes, Arthur marked its end in 1893, in The Final Problem. He died in 1930, and was interred in the churchyard at Minstead Hampshire.

Anton Chekhov

Anton Pavlovich Chekhov, the famous literary figure and Russian author, is considered one of the greatest playwrights of the modern era. He received the Pushkin Prize for his outstanding contributions to plays and short stories. He produced some of the famous comedies and tragedies of his time.

INTERESTING FACT

In his school days, Chekhov used to go to the theatre in disguise wearing a false beard, makeup and glasses.

Early Life

Anton Pavlovich Chekhov was born in Taganrog, Russia on January 17, 1860. Chekhov used to work in his father's store and sing in church as a child. Chekhov's father went bankrupt when he was 15 years old. Chekhov left home and gave private tuition to finish his schoolwork. Chekhov was awarded a scholarship to the Moscow University Medical School in 1879. Chekhov earned his Medical Doctorate in 1884.

Work

His first story was published in the Dragonfly magazine in March 1880. *The Tales of Melpomene,* his first book, was a collection of six humour pieces and was released in 1884. Chekhov soon began writing serious fiction and dramas. Chekhov's most famous plays include *The Sea Gull, Uncle Vanya, The Wood Demon,* and *The Cherry Orchard.*

Later Life

Chekov suffered from tuberculosis in his later years. Despite his illness, he continued to participate in his plays' production. Chekov passed away on July 14, 1904, at the age of forty-four. He died in a German health resort and was buried in Moscow.

George Eliot

One of the most famous novelists of the Victorian era, Mary Anne Evans, wrote under the pseudonym George Eliot. Her primary goal in choosing a male name for her writings was to increase the likelihood that they would be published. She was aware that a man's words are more frequently accepted than a woman's in patriarchal societies.

Early Life

Mary Ann Evans was born in Nuneaton, Warwickshire, England, on November 22, 1819. She met Maria Lewis in Coventry, who inspired her with her knowledge and teachings. Young Mary was an excellent student and voracious reader. When Mary was 16, her mother died, and she was forced to return home to take care of the household. When Mary was 21, her brother married and took over the family home, and Mary and her father moved to Foleshill, near Coventry.

INTERESTING FACT

After the success of her first novel, *Adam Bede*, Eliot was forced to reveal her gender because many men claimed to have written it.

Work

Scenes of Clerical Life, her first collection of stories, was published in 1858. She published it under a male pseudonym, George Eliot because writing was a male-dominated profession at the time. Her first novel, *Adam Bede,* was published soon after. Her major works include *The Mill on the Floss, Silas Marner,* and *Middlemarch.*

Later Life

Mary married her friend, John Walter Cross, in 1880. Mary died on December 22, 1880, barely seven months after her marriage. She was laid to rest in the Highgate Cemetery in London.

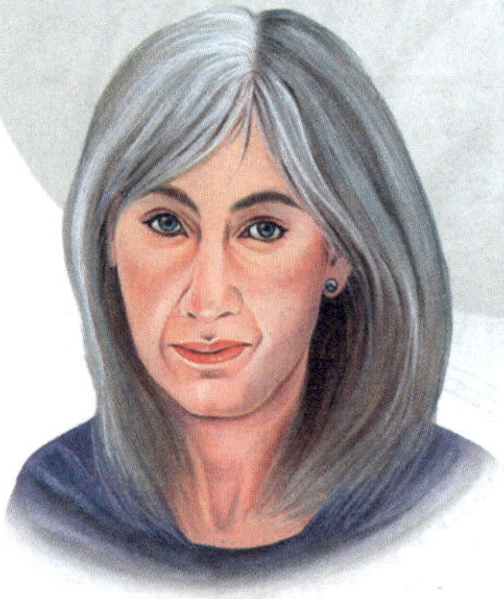

J.K. Rowling

J.K. Rowling is a British author best known for creating the popular character, Harry Potter. Her books are admired by children, and in 1998, she made the best-seller list. Her *Harry Potter* fantasy series won her numerous awards, and she rose to international fame as a writer.

Life

J.K. Rowling was born in Yate, Gloucestershire, England on July 31, 1965. Rowling attended Exeter University in Paris after graduating from Wyedean Comprehensive School to study French and the classics. She married Jorge Arantes, a Portuguese television journalist while working as a teacher in Portugal. The marriage, however, did not last long, and Rowling returned to England with her infant daughter.

Work

While sitting on a delayed train from Manchester to London in 1990, she had the idea for a story about a young boy attending a school of wizardry. Rowling finished her first novel in 1995. She based her characters on the real-life people she had been meeting since she was a child. After being rejected by several publishers, her book *Harry Potter and the Sorcerer's Stone* was finally published in June 1997 by Bloomsbury.

Harry Potter

J.K. Rowling's wizarding world captivated readers all over the world. The books received numerous honours and awards, including the Nestlé Smarties Book Prize. The series' final four books have set records for the fastest-selling books in history. Rowling rose to multi-millionaire status in just five years. The films based on the seven-book series have also been huge hits.

INTERESTING FACT

Rowling's first book was 'Rabbit' which she wrote at the age of six.

C.S. Lewis

Clive Staples Lewis, also known by his pen name C.S. Lewis, is a well-known author of English literature. He is renowned as a talented novelist, essayist, and critic. He was a very successful children's book author best known for his book *Chronicles of Narnia.*

Early Life

Lewis was born in Belfast, Ireland, on November 29, 1898. Lewis received his early education at home. Lewis was a passionate writer and an avid reader. Lewis was given a scholarship in 1916, allowing him to enrol in Oxford's university college. He earned degrees in English language and literature, philosophy, ancient history, and Greek and Latin literature.

INTERESTING FACT

C.S. Lewis was extremely bad at mathematics.

Later Life

Lewis endured a great deal of suffering in his later years, first from his wife's illness and then from his own. His wife, whom he had married in 1956, passed away from cancer in 1960. Later, in 1963, his health deteriorated, and he left Cambridge. Lewis passed away in November of the same year.

Work

Lewis received an offer to teach at Oxford's Magdalen College shortly after receiving his degree in 1924. He accepted the offer, stayed there until 1955, and then began instructing at Cambridge. He published two poems: *Spirits in Bondage* (1919) and *Dymer* (1926), which were followed by *The Pilgrim's Regress,* his first theological work. Lewis quickly rose to prominence in a group of authors responsible for classic works like *The Lord of the Rings* and *The Space Trilogy. Out of the Silent Planet,* the first book in *The Space Trilogy* was later released in 1938. As a result of their success, he wrote the seven-book *The Chronicles of Narnia* series.

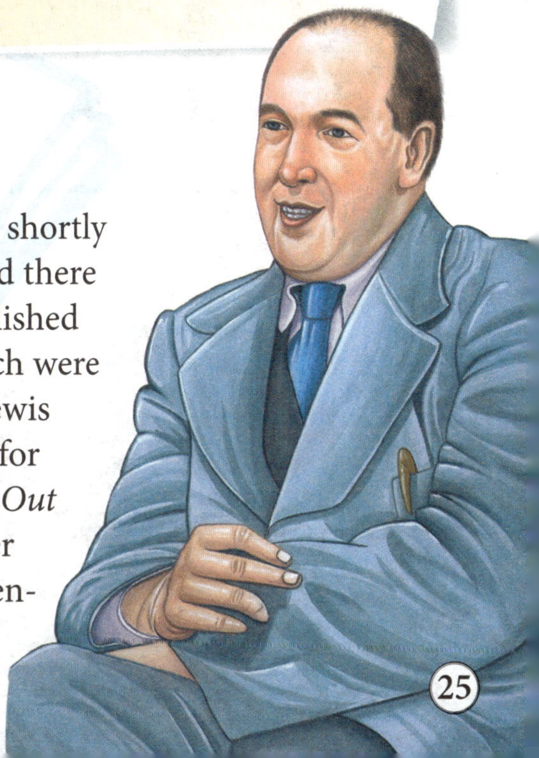

Charlotte Brontë

Charlotte Bronte was an English writer who became popular with the success of her novel Jane Eyre. She, along with her two sisters, Emily and Anne Bronte, produced some of the most astounding novels that subsequently became the benchmarks in English Literature.

Early Life

Charlotte Bronte was the third child of Patrick and Maria Bronte and was born on April 21, 1816. Charlotte's two elder sisters died as a result of the harshness, indifference, and unhealthy food at their school. Charlotte and her remaining siblings used to write stories about their fictitious world, Angria. Charlotte began to write stories regularly, such as *The Search for Happiness* and *Reader, I Married Him*. Charlotte attended Roe Head School in 1831, where she met her lifelong friend Ellen Nussey.

INTERESTING FACT

Charlotte's debut book, *The Professor*, was released three years after her death by Elizabeth Gaskell.

Work

After completing her studies in 1832, Charlotte began her career as a teacher in 1835. The Bronte sisters published a book of poems in 1846. Later, Charlotte began writing novels, and she published her first two books under the pseudonym Currer Bell. Publishers didn't want to publish her first book. Her second book, *Jane Eyre,* was released in 1847 and was a huge success. Later, in 1849, she wrote *Shirley,* and in 1853, *Villette.*

Her Marriage and Death

Charlotte Bronte married Arthur Bell Nicholls, her father's priest, on June 29, 1854. She died on March 31, 1855, at the age of 38. Bronte was laid to rest at Haworth's Church of St Michael and All Angels.

Glossary

Addison's Disease: Addison's is a disorder when your adrenal glands don't make sufficient hormones that are required to maintain blood pressure, and water and salt balances

Apprentice: Working as a trainee under someone

Astounding: Impressive to the extent that someone would wonder

Autobiographer: Someone who writes about his own life

Avid reader: Someone excessively interested in reading

Caucasus: The mountainous area in the southern region of russia

Chawton: A village in the district of hampshire, england

Civil war: A war between different groups of the same nation

Confined: To keep within boundaries or limited

Discrimination: Unfair treatment of any individual based on race, class, caste or any other reason

Enormous: A large amount or size

Halley's Comet: A short-period comet that appears every 75-76 years and is visible from Earth

Inseparable companion: Sharing a close bond with someone that one cannot live without other or cannot afford to be separated

Lieutenant: An official rank in the military

Logician: A person who studies or teaches logic

Massacre: Killing a large number of people

Mischievous: A disobedient and undisciplined child

Neurological disorder: A disorder related to the nervous system

Nobel laureate: A person awarded a nobel prize

Patriarchal society: A society where males dominate over females

Periodicals: A publication including magazines, books, or a newspaper that appears at a fixed interval

Spokesman: Someone who speaks on behalf of poor

Stammer: A speech disorder where a person repeats several sounds while speaking

Theological: Related to a god or religious practices

Worsened: Becoming worse or being deteriorated

Great Painters

Introduction

Painting, as an activity, possesses an intrinsically divine character. Throughout art history, paintings have consistently fulfilled a dual purpose. Firstly, they offer a canvas for the artist to create a novel universe, enticing us to delve into its complexities. Secondly, they serve as a sanctuary for the spectator, providing a respite from the tedium of everyday life. All great painters, regardless of their divergent perceptions, mediums, or eras, share a common attribute. This attribute is their ability to manipulate colours, crafting an aesthetically pleasing haven for us to inhabit. It is this distinct talent that earns them the honorific title of 'Great'.

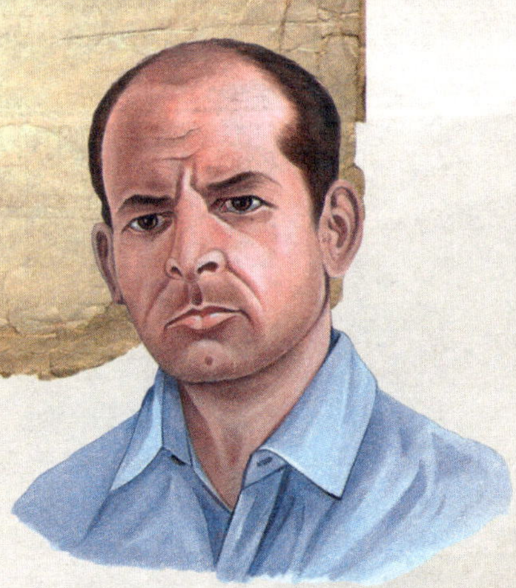

Leonardo da Vinci

Leonardo da Vinci is considered as one of the greatest painters ever lived. His creative mind and genius are widely acknowledged in the form of his paintings but he also made significant contributions to fields such as engineering, invention, architecture, and astronomy.

Early Life

Born on February 15, 1452, in Vinci, Italy, Leonardo was the son of a local lawyer, Ser Piero, and a peasant woman, Caterina. His early interest in painting led his father to send him to Florence as an apprentice to artist Verrocchio.

His Paintings

In Milan, Leonardo became the Duke's personal artist. During his 17-year stay, he completed his renowned works, *The Last Supper* and *Mona Lisa* and also made significant strides as a military engineer and inventor, observing science intently and sketching designs for various modern devices.

Other works

Leonardo is celebrated for his contribution to various fields of astronomy, aeronautics, physics, and botany. His notebooks, filled with designs like helicopters, tanks, mechanical calculators, and swinging bridges, proves his inventiveness. As a scientist, he produced numerous anatomical sketches of the human body.

INTERESTING FACT

Leonadro's studies are recorded in his notebooks which consist of 13,000 pages of notes and drawings.

Raphael

Renowned as Raphael, Raffaello Sanzio da Urbino was a distinguished Italian painter and architect. His remarkable works set the standard for Renaissance art, placing him among acclaimed painters like Michelangelo and Leonardo da Vinci.

Early life

Born in Urbino, Italy, on April 6, 1483, Raphael, son of court painter Giovanni Santi, naturally gravitated towards painting. Orphaned by age 11, his paternal uncle raised him. His early artistic training took place in Perugia under Pietro Perugino. In 1504, he relocated to Florence, where he absorbed the styles of Leonardo and Michelangelo, refining his approach to Florentine art.

INTERESTING FACT

Raphael's *Portrait of a Young Man* was one of the three paintings that were seized by the Nazis in 1939 from the Czartoryski Museum in Poland.

His work and contributions

By 1501, Raphael was recognised as a genius artist. He received his first commissions from the Church of Saint Nicholas of Tolentino in 1503, and in the following year, created his notable work, *Mond de Crucifixion.* In Florence, he produced *Deposition of Christ*. His career apexed in Rome around 1508, when Pope Julius II commissioned him to paint rooms in the Vatican Palace, housing some of Italy's most significant art.

Death

Raphael, the celebrated Italian painter and architect, died on April 6, 1520 in Rome on his 37th birthday.

Caravaggio

Michelangelo Merisi da Caravaggio, better known as Caravaggio, was a famous Italian baroque painter. His paintings are the best examples of realistic portrayals of human life.

Early life

Born on September 29, 1573, in Caravaggio, Caravaggio was the son of architect-decorator Fermo Merisi and Lucia Aratori. He apprenticed under Simone Peterzano, a student of the renowned Italian painter Titian. Later, Caravaggio worked with celebrated painter and art dealer Cesare d'Arpino, producing notable works including *Boy Peeling a Fruit, Boy with a Basket of Fruit,* and *Young Sick Bacchus.*

Later Life and Death

Despite his religious artwork, Caravaggio led a tumultuous life marked by numerous arrests and escapes. In 1606, after killing a man in a brawl, he fled to Naples, only to relocate again to Malta. Here, he created one of his acclaimed pieces, *The Beheading of St. John the Baptist*. Plagued by a severe illness in Malta, he succumbed to fever at 36.

His famous Works

Caravaggio's early notable works include such as *The Musicians* and *The Fortune Teller.* He decorated the Contarelli Chapel in the French Church of Rome with scenes from St. Matthew's life. He subsequently acquired esteemed contracts, many of which were religious works. His masterpieces include: Three paintings of St. Matthew, *The Supper at Emmaus, Death of the Virgin,* and the painting of *Cardinal's Casino 'dell' Aurora.*

INTERESTING FACT

In his entire life, Caravaggio signed only one of his paintings *La Decollazione di San Giovanni Battista.* (The Beheading of Saint John The Baptist)

Claude Monet

Claude Monet, a pivotal figure in art history, is revered as the progenitor of French Impressionism. This movement saw artists drawing inspiration from nature and utilising vibrant light and colours in their work. The term 'Impression' is derived from Monet's seminal painting, 'Impression, Sunrise'.

Early life

Born to grocer Claude-Adolphe and Louise-Justine Aubrée Monet in Paris on November 14, 1840, Oscar-Claude Monet moved to Saint-Adresse in 1845. Monet's artistic focus turned to outdoor painting under the influence of Eugène Boudin. In 1859, he joined Académie Suisse. He later worked with Boudin and Dutch painter Johan Barthold Jongkind in Le Havre, before returning to Paris in 1862 to study under Swiss artist Charles Gleyre.

INTERESTING FACT

Monet's father wanted him to join the family grocery business but he wanted to be an artist just like his mother who was a singer.

His Work

In 1865, Monet unveiled two notable works at the Salon, including *The Woman in the Green Dress* featuring his future wife, Camille Doncieux, in 1866. In the Netherlands,1871, he created twenty-five paintings. Monet painted one of his most significant works, *Impression, Sunrise* depicting a Le Havre port landscape in 1872.

His later life

In the later years, Monet immersed himself in his paintings and produced some of the great pieces. In 1879, Camille Monet died of tuberculosis. Monet painted his wife on her deathbed. On December 5, 1926, Monet breathed his last. He died of lung cancer and was interred at Giverny church cemetery.

Edgar Degas

Edgar Degas was a famous French painter and sculptor. His drawings and paintings of dancers and Parisian Street scenes earned him a place among the great artists of his time.

Early life

Edgar, born into a wealthy French banking family on July 19, 1834, was the eldest of five children. After graduating from Lycée Louis-le-Grand School in 1853, he attended the École des Beaux-Arts in 1855, studying drawing under French artist Louis Lamothe. From 1856, he spent three years in Italy honing his skills in classical art. His aspiration to explore modern art and innovative techniques was realised with the onset of the Impressionist movement in 1865.

INTERESTING FACT

In 1832, Degas's father, Auguste, changed the family name to De Gas so that it would appear elite. However, Degas went back to the original spelling in the 1860s.

His Work

Edgar, who considered himself more of a realist than an Impressionist, preferred working in his studio over nature-inspired settings, even though his work closely aligns with Impressionism. His paintings frequently depict theatrical subjects, such as racecourses, theatres, cafés, music halls, and boudoirs. Best known as the *painter of dancers*, some of his standout works are themed around dance, including *The Belleli Family, Head of a Young Woman,* and *Estelle Muson.*

Later Life

During 1880's, Edgar began loosing his eyesight. This made him indulge mostly in sculpture and pastel. He became nearly blind and quit working in 1912. He breathed his last on September 27, 1917 in Paris.

Édouard Manet

Édouard Manet was a celebrated French painter and an active member of the famous impressionist group. He influenced French art with his modern subject matter and themes depicting everyday events of life.

Early Life

Born on January 23, 1832, in Paris, Manet, the eldest son of a French magistrate, had an early fascination with drawing and painting. Despite his father's hopes for a law career, Manet committed to pursuing painting after an unsuccessful attempt at entering the Naval College and a brief stint at sea. He trained under academic painter Thomas Couture for six years. This period also included explorations in art through travels to Italy, Germany, and Holland.

His Work

Manet's work, *Absinthe Drinker,* was rejected at Salon's annual exhibition in 1859. However, his "Spanish Singer" earned him praise in 1861. He stirred controversy in 1863 with *Luncheon on the Grass* and *Music in the Tuileries.* That same year, he married his piano teacher, Suzanne Leenhoff. His paintings *Olympia* and *Christ Mocked* met with a chilly reception in 1865. His last major painting, *A Bar at the Folies-Bergère,* was produced in 1882.

INTERESTING FACT

Out of 430 known works of Manet, about two-thirds are his unfinished pieces in the form of copies or sketches.

Death

He passed away in 1883, in his early fifties. He was buried in the Cimetière de Passy in Paris.

Edward Hopper

Edward Hopper was an American realist painter known for his 20th-century depictions of both everyday and extraordinary scenes. His works, including watercolours, oil paintings, and etchings, often explore themes of isolation, melancholy, and loneliness.

Early life

Edward Hopper, born on July 22, 1882 in Nyack, New York. He explored watercolour, pen-and-ink, charcoal, and oil painting. He created numerous political cartoons and self-portraits. Recognising his talent, his parents encouraged his artistic pursuits. Hopper enrolled at the New York School of Art, where he studied Commercial art and drawing. It was there that he encountered his greatest artistic influence, the renowned American painter and teacher Robert Henri.

Work

Hopper's early works, such as *Le Pavillon de Flore, Summer Interior, The Louvre in a Thunderstorm,* and *American Village,* showcased his talent. His painting *Sailing* gained recognition at the Armory Show in 1913. His skill in etching was also admired. From 1913, he worked as a commercial illustrator for almost a decade. His 1925 painting *House by the Railroad,* exhibited at the Museum of Modern Art in New York City, marked the beginning of his mature style. Hopper's paintings depict realistic scenes of sunlit streets and houses, conveying a sense of loneliness and austerity.

INTERESTING FACT

As a young Artist, Hopper longed to study in France. However, after his visit he concluded that Paris couldn't produce great impact on him.

Death

Hopper breathed his last on 15 May 1967. He died in his studio near Washington Square in New York City.

Frida Kahlo

Frida Kahlo was Mexico's most famous woman painter whose work is considered the best of Mexican art. She is widely recognised for her distinctive style, self-portraits and the themes of pain and passion.

Early life

Frida Kahlo, born on July 6, 1907, in Coyoacán, Mexico, contracted polio at six, leaving her crippled for life. Despite her desire to pursue a medical career, her dreams were shattered at eighteen due to a severe accident that resulted in multiple fractures. While attending the National Preparatory School, she met and married the renowned artist Diego Rivera in 1929. Although they divorced after ten years, they remarried the following year, remaining in a tumultuous bond until Frida's death.

INTERESTING FACT

During her life time, Frida underwent thirty-five operations.

Her interest in Paintings

Frida turned to painting after her dreams of a medical career were shattered, using her brush to depict her personal pain. Her artworks vividly portray the harsh lives of women, with 55 out of her 143 paintings being self-portraits. Influenced by indigenous Mexican tradition, her use of vibrant colours is prominent. Notable works include *Miscarriage in Detroit*, *A Few Small Nips*, *The Two Fridas*, *Self-Portrait as a Tehuana*, and *The Love Embrace of the Universe*, and *The Earth, Myself, Diego and Señor Xólotl*.

Death

Frida Kahlo passed away on July 13, 1954, one week after her forty-seventh birthday. Her cause of death is believed to be suicide.

Gustav Klimt

Gustav Klimt, an Australian artist, remained a controversial figure in art history with his sensual and erotic paintings, which were criticised by many. He also made murals, sketches, and other art objects.

Early life

Gustav Klimt, born on July 14, 1862, in Bamgarten, near Vienna. Gustav attended the University of Plastic Arts, discovering his talent. In 1883, he opened a studio with his brother Ernst and fellow student Franz Matsch. They painted murals in theatres, churches, and museums, achieving great success. In 1897, Gustav, along with Austrian artists, founded the Vienna Secession art movement. He served as its president until 1905.

INTERESTING FACT

Gustav's *Portrait of Adele Bloch-Bauer oleh* is one of the world's most expensive paintings, which was sold at US $135,000,000.

His work

Gustav's early works included decorative ceilings and murals in Sturny's Palace, the Fiume Theatre, the Spa Hotel, and the Carlsbad City Theatre. Also, at Vienna's Burgtheater and Kunsthistorisches Museum. Notable pieces are the Beethoven frieze at the Secession building, Salome, *Adele Bloch-Bauer I, Danae, Hygeia,* and *The Kiss*. Between 1907 and 1909, he painted five fur-draped society women.

Death

Gustav died on 6 February 1918 in Vienna due to pneumonia and flu. He was interred in the Hietzing Cemetery in Vienna.

Paul Jackson Pollock

Paul Jackson Pollock, the enigmatic artist, was a renowned American painter who produced groundbreaking works of modern art through innovative techniques.

Early life

Born on January 28, 1912, in Wyoming, Paul Jackson Pollock was the youngest of five sons to LeRoy Pollock and Stella May McClure. He grew up in Arizona and California, attending Los Angeles' Manual Arts High School in 1928. At 18, he moved to New York to study at the Art Students League under artist Thomas Hart Benton. Benton served as Jackson's motivation for the next decade, and he was also deeply influenced by Mexican artists José Clemente Orozco and Diego Rivera.

Work

In 1943, Jackson had his first solo exhibition at Peggy Guggenheim's Art of This Century gallery in New York. He received a contract from Guggenheim until 1947. Starting in 1944, he created abstract paintings using paint drips, becoming famous as 'Jack the Dripper.' His first solo exhibition at Studio Paul Facchetti in Paris took place in 1952.

INTERESTING FACT

Jackson's painting *No. 5, 1948* was sold for US $140 million in 2006 and is world's most expensive painting at present.

Death

Jackson was killed in a car accident on August 11, 1956 and was buried in River Cemetery in Springs New York.

John William Waterhouse

John William Waterhouse, a prominent painter in art history, is renowned for his classical and literary-themed portrayals of women from mythology and literature.

Early Life

John William Waterhouse, born on April 6, 1849, in Rome, came from a family of painters. Assisting his father, he developed a passion for art, receiving early lessons from him. He later attended the Royal Academy, initially studying sculpture but ultimately shifting his focus to painting.

Death

Waterhouse breathed his last on 10 February, 1917. He died after suffering from long and severe illness.

His Work

In 1874, Waterhouse's painting *Sleep and His Half-Brother Death* launched his success at the Royal Academy's Summer Exhibition. He was elected an associate of the academy in 1885, and a full academician in 1895. He taught at St. John's Wood Art School, joining its Art Club. His paintings of legendary female figures like *La Belle Dame Sans Merci* and *The Lady of Shalott* are among his most impactful works.

INTERESTING FACT

Waterhouse's esteem was such that even his unfinished work, *The Enchanted Garden*, was posthumously displayed at the Royal Academy exhibition.

Michelangelo

Michelangelo di Lodovico Buonarroti Simoni, commonly known as Michelangelo, was an Italian Renaissance painter who revolutionised art. In addition to painting, he showcased mastery as a sculptor, architect, engineer, and poet.

Early life

Born in Caprese, Italy, on March 6, 1475, Michelangelo was raised by his father after his mother's death at age six. Michelangelo pursued his passion for art, apprenticing under renowned painter Domenico Ghirlandaio. Surpassing Ghirlandaio, he trained under Lorenzo de' Medici, returning home upon Medici's death in 1492. He then studied anatomy on corpses, sanctioned by church prior Niccolò Bichiellini.

Work

Michelangelo, known for his early works like the wooden crucifix for Bichiellini, carved *Bacchus* in Rome and was commissioned to create 'Pietà', a renowned sculpture of Mary and Christ. His celebrated work, *David* and pieces like *Madonna and Child* highlighted his artistry. His frescoes in the Sistine Chapel, depicting Genesis and *The Last Judgment*, remain his most influential paintings.

INTERESTING FACT

From 1527 to 1529, Michelangelo took a break from his artistic career and joined army in order to defend the Republic of Florence.

Death

Michelangelo breathed his last on 18 February 1564 in Rome. He was interred as per his wish, in the Basilica di Santa Croce in Florence.

Pablo Picasso

Pablo Picasso, a renowned Spanish painter and sculptor, emerged as one of the most influential and prolific artists in the history of Western art in the 20th century.

Early life

Born in Málaga, Spain, on October 25, 1881, to painter José Ruiz Blasco, Picasso showed early artistic interest, creating his first oil painting, *The Picador*, at eight. After attending Instituto da Guarda, he joined an art school in Barcelona in 1896, later transferring to Academia San Fernando in Madrid.

INTERESTING FACT

Picasso was a born artist. It is believed that the first word he spoke as a baby was "piz," short of lápiz the Spanish word for 'pencil.'

Work

Picasso's art phases began with early works in Paris in 1900, followed by illustrating for Madrid's Arte Joven newspaper in 1901. His 1903 masterpieces include *The Soup* and *Crouching Woman*, with subsequent works inspired by a Holland trip. From 1909-1912, he focused on geometrical still lifes, evolving into Synthetic Cubism with collages (1912-1919). His later works include portraits of his future wife, Olga Koklova, and significant pieces like *Still Life with Guitar* and *The Charnel House*.

Death

Pablo Picasso breathed his last on 8 April 1973 in Mougins, France. He was buried at the Chateau of Vauvenargues near Aix-en-Provence.

Peter Paul Rubens

Flemish painter Peter Paul Rubens, known for portraits, hunt scenes, and historical paintings, also served as a scholar, art collector, and diplomat.

Early life

Born in Siegen, Westphalia, on June 28, 1577, Rubens relocated to Antwerp after his father's death. He received a humanist education and apprenticed under artists Tobias Varhaeght, Adam van Noort, and Otto van Veen. Upon becoming an independent master in 1598, he visited Italy in 1600, where he studied classical art and was inspired by Michelangelo, Raphael, and Leonardo da Vinci.

INTERESTING FACT

Rubens produced about 2000 paintings, achieved with the help of assistants who prepared basic structures, which he then finalised with his unique touch.

Work

Rubens painted renowned portraits in Italy, including *The Equestrian Portrait of the Duke of Lerma*. He returned to Antwerp in 1608 due to his mother's illness, became a court painter, and married Isabella Brant. His masterpieces include *The Raising of the Cross, The Union of Earth and Water*, and *The Battle of the Amazons*.

Death

He breathed his last on May 30, 1640 and is believed to have died due to gout. He was buried in Saint Jacob's church, Antwerp.

Salvador Dali

Twentieth-century painter Salvador Dalí distinguished himself with his mysterious, dream-like imagery, setting his work apart from contemporaries.

Early life

Born in Catalonia, Spain on May 11, 1904, Salvador Dalí was encouraged by his mother to pursue art. After her death when he was 16, Dalí moved to Madrid to study fine arts at the Academia de San Fernando. Leaving without graduating, he moved to Paris, establishing himself as an unconventional artist and joining a leading group of innovators.

INTERESTING FACT

Dali left the prestigious school, Academia de San Fernando, in between his graduation, claiming that no teacher there is experienced enough to teach him.

Work

While in Paris, Dalí produced iconic paintings like *The Persistence of Memory* and *Metamorphosis of Narcissus*. After marrying Helena Diakanoff Devulina in 1934, he expanded his influence to filmmaking, architecture, sculpture, photography, and writing, collaborating with Luis Buñuel on *Un chien andalou* and authoring *Hidden Faces*.

Death

After the death of his wife in 1982, Dali's own health deteriorated. His finals years were surrounded by numerous health problems. He died on January 23, 1989, due to heart failure.

Sandro Botticelli

The Italian Renaissance painter Sandro Botticelli contributed to Florentine art with his large-scale paintings and frescoes, uniquely emphasising spirituality over humanity.

INTERESTING FACT

Botticelli never married, and It is believed that even the idea of marriage gave him nightmares.

Early life

Born in 1445 in Florence, Alessandro Filipepi, later known as Botticelli, apprenticed under painter Fra Filippo Lippi from 1462. Proficient in wood panel and fresco painting, he opened a workshop at fifteen. He gained renown, becoming the preferred painter for the Medici royal family.

Works

Patronised by the Medici family, Botticelli painted parts of the Sistine Chapel in Rome, positioning him among Renaissance giants like Michelangelo and Perugino. Notable works like *The Adoration of the Magi, The Birth of Venus,* and *Primavera* showcase his dreamy, religious, and mythological themes. He adopted a mature style post-1490.

Death

Sandro Botticelli died in 1510 when he was at the age of 65. He was buried in the Church of Ognissanti in Florence.

Vincent Van Gogh

Vincent van Gogh, considered the greatest Dutch artist after Rembrandt, produced remarkable artworks in just ten years. Sadly, his talent was recognised posthumously, leading to his fame after his death.

Early Life

Vincent van Gogh, born on March 30, 1853, in Zundert, Netherlands, attended the village school, then was homeschooled, and later joined a boarding school. At 16, he started working for art dealer Goupil & Co., in The Hague, and was later transferred to London and Paris before being dismissed in 1876. Discovering his talent in 1880, he embarked on his painting career.

INTERESTING FACT

During his life, Vincent suffered from severe mental illness. He even spent few months in Mental asylum.

Work

Vincent van Gogh, known for painting the underprivileged, created his famous work *Potato Eaters* in 1885. Moving to Paris in 1886, he shifted his focus from the deprived to cafés and cityscapes. In Arles, he produced over 200 works, including renowned paintings like *Fishing Boats on the Beach at Saintes-Maries*, *The Night Café*, and *The Artist's Bedroom at Arles*.

Later Life

In his final years, Van Gogh painted portraits of Dr. Gachet, his daughters, and the Church of Auvers, concluding with *Wheatfield with Crows* in July 1890. He tragically ended his life on July 27, 1890.

Rembrandt

Rembrandt, a renowned Dutch painter and etcher, is a crucial figure in Dutch and European art history, celebrated for his vibrant colours and masterful brushwork.

INTERESTING FACT

Despite his success in art, he was living beyond his means and became bankrupt in 1656.

Early Life

Rembrandt Harmenszoon van Rijn, born on July 15, 1606, in Leiden, Netherlands, was the ninth child of Harmen Gerritszoon, and Neeltgen. Initially sent to the University of Leiden, his passion for painting led him to become a pupil of local master Jacob van Swanenburch and painter Pieter Lastman. Influenced by great artists like Caravaggio, he quickly excelled in his artistic pursuits and began teaching by age twenty-three.

Death

Rembrandt died, on October 4, 1669 in Amsterdam. He was interred in an unmarked grave in the Westerkerk.

Work

By 1631, Rembrandt's success led him to Amsterdam, becoming a renowned portrait painter in Holland. In 1634, he married Saskia van Uylenburgh, often depicted in his works. He excelled in portraits, landscapes, and etchings. Notable works include *Danaë, Jacob de Gheyn III, Anatomy Lesson of Dr. Nicolaes Tulp, Six's Bridge, Syndics of the Drapers Guild,* and *Night Watch.*

Glossary

Anatomy: study of the structure of a human body

Apprentice: working as a trainee under someone

Assimilated: taking up or learning something

Baroque Painter: a painter was produces paintings having elaborate ornamentation in decorative art, commonly known as baroque paintings

Caricaturist: a person who draws exaggerated portraits of people or objects in order to produce comic effects

Commercial Illustrator: an artist that works for any company, commonly advertising, and creates art for commercial purposes

Contemporaries: people or artist living at the same time

Court Painter: an artist that works as a painter for royal families

Cubism: an artistic movement in the early 20th Century characterised by the depiction of simplified planes, lines and geometric structures

Etchings: a technique of creating art on the surface of glass or metal plate

flemish painter: an artist who is related to the culture or language of Belgium

Fresco: a method of painting done on wet plasters on walls or ceilings

Gold Engraver: a skilled worker who engraves or carves designs on gold

Gout: a painful disorder caused by the deposits of uric acid in the joints

Isolation: a state of being alone, away from everyone

Melancholy: a state of depression or misery

Pelvis: a large bony structure at the base of the spine that supports the legs

Perspective: point of view

Prior: The head of a religious order or Church

Protestant minister: minister of a group of people who denies the authority of Pope and was against the Catholic Church

Pulmonary embolism: a blockage of the pulmonary artery by any matter

Reclusive: withdrawn from society

Rheumatism: a disorder of the joints or muscles or connective tissues leading to severe pain

Tumultuous: a noisy or turbulent relationship

Unconventional: different from the usual

Great Musicians

Introduction

Listening to music is considered the most rejuvenating experience for the human mind and soul. Several musicians throughout history have appealed to our senses with their amazing musical compositions and creativity. They used music as a mean of artistic expression and inspired people by their works. The sensational songs and compositions that these great people created keep them alive even today. From classical to rock, music has travelled a long way through the centuries. This book compiles the lives of some of the most talented and prolific musicians that have made valuable contributions to our world of music.

Wolfgang Amadeus Mozart

Wolfgang Amadeus Mozart was an Austrian music composer. He is one of the best musicians ever to have lived in the history of music. His genius surpassed the boundaries of whatever form of music he took up including classical, contemporary, instrumental and vocal.

INTERESTING FACT

Mozart's full name is Johannes Chrysostomus Wolfgangus Theophillus Amadeus Gottlieb Sigismundus Mozart.

Early Life and Education

Wolfgang Amadeus Mozart, born on January 27, 1756, in Salzburg, had a musical upbringing under his father, Leopold, a composer and violinist at the local Prince-Archbishop's court. Alongside his sister Nannerl, he embarked on musical tours to explore diverse genres. At the tender age of six, Mozart showcased his brilliance by composing and performing on the keyboard. His tours across cities like Paris and London established him as a remarkable child prodigy.

Death

During the premiere of his opera *La clemenza di Tito*, Mozart became severely ill. Tragically, he passed away on December 5th, 1791.

Professional Career

As a member of the Salzburg orchestra, he refined his skills. By 16, he had performed three operas in Milan. His groundbreaking opera, Idomeneo, in 1781 propelled his success. His years in Vienna, starting at twenty-five until his demise, epitomized a golden age of music. Mozart composed some of his finest works, working as a freelance composer, teacher, and pianist. Notable operatic creations include *The Marriage of Figaro (1786), Don Giovanni (1787)*, and *Così fan tutte (1790)*.

Ludwig van Beethoven

Ludwig van Beethoven was a famous German musician. He is widely regarded as one of the most significant figures in the history of music. Beethoven was extremely gifted and his father desired him to become a child prodigy like Mozart.

Early childhood

Ludwig van Beethoven, born on December 16th, 1770, in Bonn, Germany, had a musical upbringing. Under strict training, Beethoven's talents flourished, and by the age of seven, he astounded audiences with his brilliant performances. To refine his skills, he became a student of Christian Gottlob Neefe, and at the age of 10, he created his first composition.

Professional Career

In 1787, Beethoven embarked on a Vienna tour where Mozart praised his exceptional abilities. Sadly, Beethoven had to return to Bonn upon learning of his mother's passing. In July 1792, Beethoven returned to Vienna to study under Mozart, but Mozart's recent demise led him to Joseph Hayden. Throughout his twenties, Beethoven emerged as an outstanding pianist. In 1800, he published his first symphony, propelling his music to new heights. He composed beloved pieces like *Für Elise* and *Ode to Joy*, the European National Anthem.

INTERESTING FACT

Beethoven turned deaf when he was 30 and he composed some of his best music after that.

Death

Beethoven breathed his last on March 26, 1827. He was interred in Wahring Cemetery. Later his remains were shifted to Zentral-friedhof in Vienna.

Johann Sebastian Bach

Johann Sebastian Bach was a German composer, violinist and organist. Known for his brilliant musical pieces, he is regarded as one of the greatest composers of all time.

Early Life

Johann Sebastian Bach, born on March 31st, 1685, in Germany, displayed remarkable musical talent from a young age. At the age of nine, he tragically lost his parents and was cared for by his eldest brother, an organist. Under his brother's guidance, Bach honed his organ skills and eventually worked as an organist at Georgenkirche until 1703. During his childhood, he also learned keyboard from Johann Pachelbel.

INTERESTING FACT

When Prince, Frederick of Sweden heard Bach's music he became so impressed that he took out his diamond ring and gave it to him.

Professional Career

In 1703, Bach began his career as an organist at Kneue Kirche church. By 1707, he secured another organist position in Germany. In 1708, Bach became the organist and chamber musician for the Duke of Saxe-Weimar. During his tenure, Bach composed exquisite organ pieces. Later, he joyfully accepted an offer from Prince Leopold of Cöthen, Germany, resulting in some of his greatest instrumental works. In 1723, Bach became the choir leader in Leipzig, where he remained for life, publishing over 300 musical works.

Later Years

In the later years of his life, Bach lost his eyesight completely. He had a stroke and high fever which led to his death on July 28, 1750.

Michael Jackson

Michael Joseph Jackson also called 'moonwalker' was an American singer, songwriter and dancer. Famous for his unique style and dance style 'moonwalk', he was announced as the most popular entertainer of all time by the Guinness World Records.

Early Life

Michael Jackson was born August 29, 1958 in Gary, Indiana. His was a working class family and he was the eighth of ten children. When Michael was nearly 5, he joined a musical band formed by his elder brothers. The band was named 'The Jackson 5' and by the age of eight, he emerged as the leading voice of the band. With growing performances, the Band widely became famous and popular. In 1969, the president of Motown Records, Berry Gordy, Jr. signed the group that opened the gates of bright career for the Jackson brothers.

INTERESTING FACT

Apart from his two children with his second wife; Michael Jackson had another child, Prince Michael Jackson II.

Autobiography

In February 1988, Michael published his autobiography, *Moonwalk*. Named after his signature dance move moonwalk, the book sold over 450,000 copies in 14 countries. The book was re-released after his death on October 13, 2009.

Success

In 1978 Michael Jackson appeared in-The Wiz. The film was an African American version of *The Wizard of Oz* , an American fantasy film. With Quincy Jones, Michael did an album, *Off the Wall* in 1979. Jones and Michael again worked on Michael's album the *Thriller* (1982). The *Thriller* added much to Michael's publicity and he became the single most popular performer in America. Jackson remained in the limelight throughout the 1980's and became famous as *King of Pop* His other albums *Bad* (1987), and *Dangerous* (1991) solidified his pop star image.

Elvis Presley

Elvis Presley was an American singer who is widely popular for initiating the famous rock and roll era. Famous as the 'King of Rock 'n' Roll', Elvis is considered as the most important figure of the 20th-century popular culture. His forms included country, pop ballads, gospel, and blues.

Early Life

Born on January 8, 1935, in Tupelo, Mississippi, Elvis Presley's father faced numerous unsuccessful endeavours. During his elementary years, Elvis astounded a teacher with his singing prowess, igniting his passion. Encouraged to participate in competitions, he joined his local church choir. At the age of 13, Elvis relocated to Memphis, Tennessee, attending L. C. Humes High School and graduating in 1953. To fund his recordings, he began working as a truck driver, setting the stage for his musical journey.

Professional Career

Elvis's professional journey began with *That's All Right Mama* His first RCA release, *Heartbreak Hotel*, propelled him to international stardom. With fusing country and rock and roll, he emerged as a leading figure in the rock and roll era; he made his film debut in *Love Me Tender* (1956), starred in 33 films, and delivered electrifying live concerts. Elvis received 14 Grammy nominations and won three, along with a GrammyAward.

INTERESTING FACT

Elvis liked visiting the Funeral Home that had his mother's body. He used to sleep there on a couch and often sit there quietly the whole night.

Military service, Marriage and Death

In 1958, Elvis joined the U.S. military and served in Germany until his discharge in 1960. In 1967, he married Priscilla Beaulieu. Tragically, on August 16th, 1977, Elvis passed away from a heart attack.

Madonna

Madonna is an American singer, dancer and actress who is popular for her astonishing contributions to the entertainment industry. Known as the world's most successful female recording artist of all time by Guinness Book of World Records, Madonna has given a new meaning to the world of music.

Early Life

Madonna Louise Ciccone, born on August 16, 1958, in Bay City, Michigan, emerged as the third of six siblings. Tragically, Madonna lost her mother at the tender age of 5. Madonna attended St. Frederick's and St. Andrew's Elementary Schools before progressing to West Middle School. At Rochester Adams High School, she garnered recognition for her academic excellence. It was during this time that Madonna discovered her passion for dance, leading to a dance scholarship at the University of Michigan. Under the guidance of Christopher Flynn, her esteemed ballet instructor, her talent flourished.

Professional Career

In 1978, Madonna embarked on a journey to New York to chase her dancing dreams. She grappled with odd jobs, performed with Alvin Ailey American Dance Theater, and temporarily danced for French disco artist, Patrick Hernandez. After her return from Paris, Sire Records signed her in 1982. Her inaugural album, *Madonna,* launched in 1983, was a resounding triumph. By 1991, Madonna amassed 21 US Top Ten hits, transitioning to the silver screen with hits like *Desperately Seeking Susan*. In 2008, she joined the Rock and Roll Hall of Fame.

INTERESTING FACT

In the year 1989, Madonna's video *Like A Prayer* caused much controversy and was condemned for being abusive on the religious front.

Elton John

Elton John is an English musician who has earned a place for himself among the greatest singers and composers of all time. Famous for his flashy clothes and groundbreaking hits, Elton John is also a name among active philanthropists of the world.

Early Life

Born on March 25, 1947, in Middlesex, England, Elton John was nurtured in a musically inclined household. His talent manifested early as his young fingers gracefully manipulated the piano keys at age four. By 11, he was a scholarship recipient at the Royal Academy of Music and later studied at the London Academy. Forsaking traditional academia, John chose to pursue his musical career, performing as a pub pianist and working for a music publisher. In 1964, he joined Bluesology, a band known for showcasing talents like John Baldry and Elton Dean.

INTERESTING FACT

Elton John's original name is Reginald Kenneth Dwight. He adopted the name 'Elton John', on the names of his band's (Bluesology) saxophonist, Elton Dean, and singer, Long John Baldry, to pay homage to them.

Professional Career

In 1969, John's maiden album *Empty Sky* fell short of commercial success. However, his fortunes dramatically reversed with his second album *Your Song*, released in 1971, thrusting him into the global limelight. His rise to fame was punctuated by hits like 'Rocket Man' and 'Levon'. His eccentric style, oversized glasses, and flamboyant outfits made him a quintessential pop icon. He joined the Rock and Roll Hall of Fame in 1994 and secured an Academy Award in 1995. In 2001, he won a Grammy for 'Elton John and Tim Rice's Aida'.

Billy Joel

Billy Joel is a popular American singer and composer who is known for upholding the rock tradition in music. He stands sixth in the list of best-selling artist in the United States according to RIAA.

Early life

Born on May 9, 1949, in New York, Billy Joel was cradled in a world of classical music, influenced by his pianist father, Karl Amson Joel, and mother, Rosalind Nyman. At just four, he began exploring piano, later dabbling in boxing during adolescence. After a nose injury, Joel hung up his boxing gloves, entranced by The Beatles' performance and drawn towards a music career. By fourteen, he was part of the band Echoes, moving to *Hassles* in 1967, a collaboration disrupted due to Joel's affair with the drummer's wife.

Professional Career and success

In 1971, Joel debuted with his solo album *Cold Spring Harbor*, which underperformed. Distressed, Joel and his girlfriend Elizabeth Weber journeyed to Los Angeles, where he performed in piano bars under the pseudonym Bill Martin. His song *Captain Jack*, caught Columbia Records' attention in 1973, leading to the release of his breakthrough hit, *Piano Man*. His success escalated, culminating in a Grammy for *Just the Way You Are* in 1977. A pioneer, Joel introduced the tradition of music videos in 1980 and was honoured in the Rock and Roll Hall of Fame in 1999.

INTERESTING FACT

Joel once overslept on the day of one of his important exams due to his late-night musician's routine. As a result he couldn't complete his graduation.

The Rolling Stones

The Rolling Stones are an English rock band formed in London, UK in 1962. Often considered as 'the world's greatest rock and roll band', The Rolling Stones have sold more than 200 million albums worldwide.

The formation of group

The Rolling Stones sprang from a shared passion for music between schoolmates, guitarist Keith Richards and singer Mick Jagger. Initially including Ian Stewart, Dick Taylor, Tony Chapman, and Brian Jones, the band underwent changes. Jazz drummer Charlie Watts replaced Chapman, and bassist Bill Wyman filled in for Taylor. In 1963, Andrew Loog Oldham, manager of London's Marquee Club, signed the band. At the moment of billing, they declared their name as 'Brian Jones and The Rollin' Stones'.

INTERESTING FACT

The Rolling Stones were named after an American musician, Muddy Waters' song 'Rolling Stone'. Interestingly the name came into the mind of Jones after glancing at Muddy Water's that was laying on the floor whose one of the tracks was Rolling Stone.

Early performances and Success

Securing a contract with Decca Records in June 1963, The Rolling Stones made waves with their hits *I Want to Be Loved* and *I Wanna Be Your Man*. Their fourth single, *It's All Over Now* shattered records in England. Their global hit *Satisfaction* in 1965 further cemented their fame. Following Jones' exit and subsequent tragic death in 1969, Mick Taylor joined the ensemble. The band, renowned for their global concerts and albums, was honoured with an induction into the Rock & Roll Hall of Fame in 1989.

The Beatles

The Beatles were a rock band that was formed in England in 1960. It was one of the most successful bands in the history of music.

The Success of the group

In 1963, The Beatles' hit, *Please Please Me*, paved the way for their future successes. Their memorable hits included *Yellow Submarine, Eleanor Rigby, Penny Lane*, and the celebrated *Sergeant Peppers Lonely Hearts Club Band*. They also starred in films like *A Hard Day's Night, Help!, and Yellow Submarine.*

INTERESTING FACT

The Beatles have been honored with 7 Grammy Awards and 15 Ivor Novello Awards from the British Academy of Songwriters, Composers and Authors.

Formation of The Beatles

In 1956, John Lennon, a student at Quarry Bank School in Liverpool, initiated *The Quarry Men*, featuring Paul McCartney, Eric Griffiths, Colin Hanton, Pete Shotton, Rod Davis, and Bill Smith, with Lennon as lead vocalist. Later, Ivan Vaughan supplanted Bill. Following several name shifts, including 'Johnny and the Moondogs' and 'the Silver Beatles', they finally settled on 'The Beatles'. EMI Records producer George Martin signed them, and Ringo Star replaced Pete. Their inaugural song, *Love Me Do*, debuted on October 5, 1962.

Break up and aftermath

In 1970, personal differences led to The Beatles' dissolution, prompting each member to embark on solo ventures. John Lennon, turned activist, was tragically murdered in 1980. In the 1990s, George Harrison, sadly, succumbed to cancer on November 29, 2001.

Aretha Franklin

Aretha Louise Franklin was an American singer and is regarded as the most influential female artist of all time. In 1987 Aretha emerged as the first woman inducted into the Rock and Roll Hall of Fame. Also, as a winner of 18 competitive Grammys and two honorary Grammys she is one of the most esteemed artists by the Grammy awards.

His Early life

Born on March 25, 1942, in Memphis, Tennessee, Aretha Franklin faced her parents' separation at six, then was raised by her grandmother and Baptist minister father. Tragedy struck at ten with her mother's death. In her early teens, Aretha's vocals graced her father's church, and she journeyed with him to gospel programs nationwide. With mentoring from gospel luminaries like Clara Ward, Albertina Walker, and Mahalia Jackson, she blossomed into a vocal prodigy. At 14, her debut album, *Songs of Faith*, was released. Supported by her father, she transitioned to secular music.

INTERESTING FACT

In 2005, Aretha became the second woman, after Madonna, to be inducted into the UK Music Hall of fame.

Professional Career and Success

Relocating to New York City, Aretha was aided by Columbia Records executive John Hammond in securing a recording contract. Her musical prowess, evident from her hit classic *Today I Sing the Blues*, spanned various genres from Broadway ballads to youth-oriented rhythm and blues. Critics adored her, but mainstream success eluded her until her collaboration with Atlantic Records in 1966. Producers Jerry Wexler and Arif Mardin assisted her rise to stardom. Her influential 1960s R&B recordings, like *I Never Loved a Man (The Way I Love You)*, led to a slew of Top Ten hits, including *Chain of Fools* and *Think*.

Bob Dylan

Bob Dylan, born as Robert Allen Zimmerman, is an American singer. Often known as the Shakespeare of his generation, he revolutionised music with his contributions and made a long-lasting impact.

Early Life

Bob Dylan, born May 24, 1941 in Duluth, Minnesota, developed a penchant for music early on. As a high school student, he joined several bands, including 'The Shadow Blasters' and 'The Golden Chords'. In 1959, his university years in Minneapolis sparked a deeper fascination with American folk music, leading to performances at the local coffee house, 10 O'Clock Scholar.

INTERESTING FACT

Dylan has published three books of drawings and paintings and his work has been exhibited in major art.

Professional Career and Success

Bob Dylan was born in 1962, Through hits such as *The Freewheelin' Bob Dylan* and *Blowin' in the Wind*, Dylan established himself as a star. After several folk albums, he pivoted to folk-rock with the 1965 release of *Bringing It All Back Home*. Expanding his creative horizons, Dylan ventured into film, appearing in 'Pat Garrett and Billy the Kid' in 1973.

Achievements and Awards

Inducted into the Rock & Roll Hall of Fame in 1989, Dylan became the first to receive Kennedy Center Honors in 1997, and his album *Time Out of Mind* bagged him three Grammy Awards, including Album of the Year. In 2000, Dylan's contribution to the film 'Wonder Boys', a track titled *Things Have Changed*, earned him both a Golden Globe and an Academy.

Jimi Hendrix

Jimmi Hendrix was an American guitarist. Often regarded as the best electric guitar player ever, he is one of the most influential musicians of his generation. His music surpassed most of the genres including blues, hard rock, modern jazz, and soul.

Professional Career and Success

Leaving army life, by 1964, Jimi was making waves in Harlem's club scene, even winning a contest at The Apollo Theatre. His 1967 *Are You Experienced?*, was a groundbreaking success. The following album, *Axis: Bold as Love*, showcased Jimi's songwriting talents. His reimagined style in *Electric Ladyland* is considered his ultimate masterpiece. Later he formed the Band of Gypsys with Billy Cox.

INTERESTING FACT

In 1961, Jimi was punished for riding a stolen car and to avoid imprisonment, he joined army. His army life was as chaotic as Jimi himself was. He was often found sleeping during the duty and couldn't even use the gun properly.

Early Life

Born as Johnny Allen Hendrix on November 27, 1942, in Seattle, Washington, Jimi's father later changed his name to James Marshall Hendrix. His father took sole custody after his parents divorced when he was nine. From a young age, Jimi's heart was set on playing the guitar. Beginning with a broomstick and a one-stringed ukulele, his passion was rewarded when his father bought him a real guitar. Completely absorbed, he honed his skills by observing icons like Chuck Berry and Elvis Presley.

Death

Jimi died on September 18, 1970 leaving his album First Rays of the New Rising Sun incomplete. The reason of his death was an overdose of sleeping pills.

Ray Charles

Ray Charles Robinson Sr. was a former American musician who was widely popular for his contributions to various genres of music, including soul, pop, gospel, and blues. Despite his blindness, he established an entirely different standard of music, giving it new meaning and form.

Early Life

Born in Albany, Georgia, on September 23, 1932, Ray Charles Robinson relocated to Greenville, Florida. Tragically, Charles became completely blind at age seven. From 1937 to 1945, he attended Saint Augustine School for the Blind in Florida, where he nurtured his musical prowess, mastering the piano, clarinet, and saxophone. Heartbreak struck at ten when he lost his father, and again at fifteen when his mother passed, leaving him orphaned.

Professional Career

In 1952-53, he had recorded the boogie-woogie classic *Mess Around* and the catchy *It Should've Been Me*. His powerful rendition of Guitar Slim's *The Things That I Used to Do* became a bestseller in 1953. Signing with Atlantic Records in 1954, Charles shone in hits like *I've Got a Woman* and *Hallelujah I Love You So*.

INTERESTING FACT

Charles had a fear that people might mistake him for boxing champion Ray Robinson, thus he dropped his last name, 'Robinson', and became known as Ray Charles.

Achievements and Awards

Charles is the winner of 13 Grammy Awards, including a lifetime achievement award that he received in 1987.

Prince

Prince Rogers Nelson, better known as Prince, was an American musician. Despite his singing, Prince was an excellent guitarist, pianist and song composer. According to Robert Larsen's book History of Rock and Roll, Prince is regarded as "one of the most talented and commercially successful pop musicians of the last 20 years".

Early Life

Prince, born June 7, 1958, in Minneapolis, Minnesota, gravitated towards music, raised in a family of musicians – his father a pianist, his mother a jazz singer. He discovered his musical talents early, playing piano from age seven. By fourteen, he had joined his first band, 'Grand Central', showcasing his skills on guitar and piano while attending Minneapolis's Central High School.

INTERESTING FACT

In 1993, Prince adopted a symbol, combining male and female gender symbols with an arrow, as his name – "The Love Symbol" or "The Artist Formerly Known as Prince." He changed his name again in 2000 and came back to his original name 'Prince'.

Professional Career

At just 17, Prince signed a three-album contract facilitated by Minneapolis businessman Owen Husney. His debut album *For You* launched in 1978, followed by his eponymous album, Prince, became a resounding success. His breakthrough moment arrived in 1983 with *Little Red Corvette*, an instant crossover hit captivating millions. His acclaimed album *Purple Rain* (1984) further elevated his status as one of the 1980s' most influential stars. Prince continually produced captivating hits, securing widespread recognition in his homeland, Britain, and across Europe.

Achievements and Awards

Prince had over 30 nominations in Grammy awards out of which he is a holder of seven Grammys. the Grammy Hall of Fame.

Led Zeppelin

Led Zeppelin were an English rock band that was formed in 1968. Despite its diverse musical style, the group is regarded best for its heavy metal and hard rock style.

Formation

In 1968, the band initially known as the New Yardbirds was established by lead guitarist Jimmy Page. Alongside him were bassist John Paul Jones, drummer John Bonham, and vocalist Robert Plant. The band debuted live on 7 September 1968, and a month later, recorded their first album. Because of legal challenges on 14 October 1968, they re-emerged as Led Zeppelin. Their first performance under the new moniker was on 25 October 1968, with their debut album 'Led Zeppelin' being released on 12 January 1969.

INTERESTING FACT

In their concert in 2007, London, Bonham's son, Jason, played the drums.

Break up

Drummer, John Bonham died on 24 September, 1980. After the death of Bohman, the remaining members mutually decided to disband the group. After their break up, the group re-formed on few occasions and performed in 1985 for the Live Aid benefit, 1988 on Atlantic Records.

Early Success

Led Zeppelin's debut album with its heavy metal music caused a sensation. Their follow-up album amplified the band's popularity, topping charts in the US and UK. Live concerts and the release of *Led Zeppelin III* only enhanced their reputation. The fourth album, which remained unnamed, featured their iconic track *Stairway to Heaven*. The band continued to produce hit after hit, making them one of the most commercially successful and influential groups of the 1970s.

Pink Floyd

Pink Floyd were a British rock band widely famous for its rock music. Also known as the Tea Set, the band emerged as one of the most commercially successful groups.

Formation of the Band

Pink Floyd originated when Roger Waters and Nick Mason, studying at Regent Street Polytechnic in London, joined a band that included Keith Noble, Clive Metcalfe, Sheilagh Noble, and friend Richard Wright. Initially named 'Sigma 6', the lineup featured Wright on rhythm guitar, Waters on lead, and Mason on drums, with songwriting assistance from Ken Chapman. The band later welcomed Bob Klose as a guitarist and rebranded as The Tea Set. After Metcalfe and Noble departed to form a separate band, Syd Barrett stepped in as lead guitarist and, in 1965, rechristened the group as Pink Floyd.

INTERESTING FACT

Nick Mason, the drummer is the only member of the band to have been with the band for its entirity.

Awards

Pink Floyd boasts prestigious accolades including a BAFTA for 'Best Original Song' and 'Best Sound' in 1982, a Grammy for 'Rock Instrumental Performance' in 1995.

Success

After receiving EMI's £5,000 advance, Pink Floyd's first hit, *Arnold Layne*, was released on March 11th, 1967, followed by their debut album, *The Piper at the Gates of Dawn*, heightening their popularity. By 1968, due to Barrett's schizophrenia, Gilmour replaced him as the guitarist. Their subsequent songs *Atom Heart Mother (1970)* and *Meddle (1971)* dominated American charts. Their 1973 album *Dark Side of the Moon* was a commercial success, followed by *Wish You Were Here* in 1975.

Queen

Queen are a British rock band formed in London in 1970 by Freddie Mercury, Brian May and Roger Taylor, later joined by John Deacon. It is considered as one of the most talented, sensational and popular bands in musical history.

Formation and Early Career

In 1968, Brian May and Tim Staffell, formed a band named 'Smile' with Roger Taylor, a dental student. Staffell soon departed, and Freddie Mercury joined, recommending the new name "Queen". By 1971, the final member, bassist John Deacon, was enlisted, prompting the recording of their debut album. Their early tracks, including *Liar, Keep Yourself Alive, The Night Comes Down* and *Jesus*, were recorded for a demo tape.

INTERESTING FACT

The Queen logo also known as the Queen Crest, was designed by Mercury. The logo featured the Zodiac signs of all four members.

Awards

The 'Queen' received Seven Ivor Novello Awards. They were also inducted into the Rock & Roll Hall of Fame and Songwriters Hall of Fame.

Success

Queen's debut album made a remarkable impact, earning 'superb' accolades from Rolling Stone Magazine. Their follow-up topped the UK charts and clinched fifth place in the US. Initially embracing a progressive rock style, they gradually turned more mainstream. The band sold over 170 million albums globally, boasting 18 chart-topping albums and 10 number one DVDs. With an impressive record.

Glossary

Bass Guitar: a guitar with six strings tuned to produce low notes

Clarinet: a single reed musical instrument with a cylindrical tube

Classical Music: conventional music that has its roots in the traditions of Western liturgical and secular music

Commercial: intended to be popular and make profit

Composer: a person who composes music as a profession

Concert: a musical performance given in public

Genre: a genre in music refers to a particular type of music that can be easily differentiated from other types

Grammy Award: awards presented by the National Academy of Recording Arts and Sciences of the United States for outstanding achievements in the music industry

Homage: honor or respect shown publicly

Imprisonment: to remain in captivity

Incline: have a tendency or willingness to do something

Induct: admit someone to a group or organization

Influential: some with the power to influence someone

Interred: to bury a body after death

Jazz: a type of music that emerged in America in the beginning of the 20th century

Notable: important; worthy of attention

Outrageous: shocking, unusual

Philanthropist: someone who seeks to promote the welfare of others

Pop Ballad: slow love songs

Pro: a professional

Prodigy: a young child usually talented or gifted with exceptional qualities

Pseudonym: a fictitious name

Renowned: famous, well known

Revolutionise: bring in drastic changes

Rock: a form of popular music that emerged in the mid- and late 1960s

Saxophone: a musical instrument made of metal and belonging to the family of wind instruments such as flute etc.

Significant: important

Surpass: exceed; to be better than

Symphony: a long and complex music composition usually written for the orchestra

Tradition: an artistic style established by an artist and later followed by others

Tremendous: extremely good; in a large scale

Vocalist: a singer

Great Scientists

Introduction

Imagine how different our lives would be today if there were no electricity, telephones, or other devices that eliminated the need for human labour. Where did all of these innovations that improve and simplify our lives come from? Scientists are the creative and gifted individuals who discovered these devices. Many well-known scientists have made their mark with brilliant ideas throughout history. They provided us with machines and an abundance of crucial information. They spent many years studying various topics to unlock many of the mysteries of the universe. All of their research provided us with fascinating and life-altering information.

Aristotle

Aristotle was a great Greek philosopher and scientist. He was interested in biology and worked hard to categorise plants and animals into different groups. Aristotle was Plato's student and Alexander the Great's mentor.

His Life and Education

Aristotle was born in 384 BC to Nicomachus, a doctor at the royal court, in the Greek town of Stagira, Chalcidian League (city of Macedonia). When Aristotle was 17, he enrolled in Plato's Academy in Athens and completed his education there. As a gifted student and learner, he quickly began teaching at the academy, where he remained for the next 20 years. He returned to Macedonia after Plato's death, where he married Pythias, the King's niece. Later, he was appointed as Alexander the Great's official tutor. Alexander used to bring samples of various plants and animals from the territories he had conquered, which aided him in the creation of the world's first botanical garden. Later, Aristotle returned to Athens and established the Lyceum. He spent the remainder of his life in school, participating in various research and writing programmes.

INTERESTING FACT

Aristotle gave an account of 500 animals in his writings, including 120 different species of fish and 60 different types of insects.

Aristotle, a great scientist

Aristotle studied a variety of scientific disciplines, and explained why an object behaves a certain way in physics. He provided four causes—material, efficient, formal, and final—in this regard. In Metaphysics, he investigated the idea that every animal and plant has a soul that helps them move. In his book *On the Soul*, he provided explanations of how all living things work. Along with the four other common elements of water, fire, earth, and air, he also added the fifth element, aether, to the composition of matter.

Archimedes

Archimedes was a well-known Greek mathematician. His inventions in the fields of geometry, engineering, and science earned him prominence worldwide. He created many machines that reduced the strain of labour.

His Life and Education

Archimedes was born in Syracuse, on the island of Sicily, in 287 BC. His father was a professional astronomer. Not much is known about his childhood. He went to school in Alexandria, Egypt, and returned to Sicily after finishing his primary education in Egypt. Archimedes immersed himself in various inventions after his return. He used to get so caught up in his work that he frequently forgot to eat. During the Second Punic War in 212 BC, he is said to have been so preoccupied with one of his works that he failed to respond when a Roman soldier inquired about the whereabouts of the General. The soldier became enraged by this and killed Archimedes.

INTERESTING FACT

Archimedes discovered Archimedes' principle while taking a bath. He ran naked through the streets, exclaiming "Eureka," which is Greek for "I have found it."

Archimedes and his inventions

Archimedes made significant contributions to geometry. He discovered the relationship between a sphere's volume and a cylinder's surface area. He also provided a formula for calculating the area of space inside a curve, invented the pulley, the Archimedean screw-pumping device, the compound pulley, and the burning mirror. He also popularised Archimedes' principle, according to which the volume of water displaced by a body is equal to the volume of the body dipped in water.

Nicolaus Copernicus

Nicolaus Copernicus was a famous Polish mathematician and astronomer. He was the first to associate mathematics and science. He became well-known for his theory about Earth's and other planets' revolutions.

INTERESTING FACT

When Nicolaus witnessed a lunar eclipse, which proved to be the foundation of his heliocentric invention.

Life and Education

Nicolaus Copernicus was born in 1473 in Torun, Poland. He attended the best schools before enrolling at Cracow University in 1491, where he studied astronomy and mathematics. He decided to become a priest on the advice of his uncle and enrolled at the University of Bologna in Italy to learn the laws of the priesthood. There, the astronomer Domenico Maria de Novara had a big impact on him. He travelled to Rome in the year 1500, where he developed his theory regarding the orbital positions of the planets.

His heliocentric model

After extensive research and observation, Nicolaus put forth his theory, known as the heliocentric model. He claimed through the model that the sun is the centre of the universe and that Earth and all other planets revolve around it. He also mentioned that the Earth rotates on its axis once a day and once a year around the sun.

Galileo Galilei

Galileo Galilei, an Italian scientist, is often referred to as the "Father of Science." His efforts to develop the fundamentals of modern science were highly successful.

Life and Education

Galileo Galilei was born in Pisa, Italy, on February 15, 1564. Galileo's father encouraged him to study medicine at Pisa University. He did not, however, continue with medicine and instead studied mathematics and physics. In 1589, he was appointed as a mathematics professor at the University of Pisa, the same university where he had been denied a degree. After three years, he was hired as a mathematics professor at Padua University.

INTERESTING FACT

Around 1603, Galileo devised a thermometer which was called the "thermoscope".

Discoveries in physics

His work on kinematics, a branch of mechanics that studies the motion of a body, was his most significant contribution. He stated that a body's total distance travelled is proportional to the square of time. He concluded after much observation that a pendulum swung at a constant speed regardless of its amplitude. This pendulum law was eventually used to regulate clocks.

Astronomical discoveries

He discovered four satellites orbiting Jupiter using an improved version of the telescope. He noticed that the Moon's surface was not smooth but rough. He carried out various experiments and backed Copernicus' heliocentric model. This led to several issues, and he had to stand trial before being placed under house arrest.

Edward Jenner

Edward Jenner, the English surgeon, is known as the "Father of Immunology." His famous discovery of smallpox vaccination was a huge medical breakthrough that saved countless lives, and this groundbreaking discovery liberated the world from this lethal disease.

Life and education

Edward Jenner was born in 1749 in England. He learned his trade as an apprentice under a local surgeon named Daniel Ludlow for eight years. Later, he went to St. George's Hospital in London for brief training under a prominent surgeon, John Hunter. Following this crucial training, he returned to his hometown and established himself as a successful medical practitioner in Berkeley.

Vaccination

As a physician, Jenner noticed that patients who worked with cattle and had been exposed to the much milder illness known as cowpox were never given the smallpox diagnosis. He came up with a method to expose a cowpox vaccine recipient to smallpox. There was no smallpox infection in the individual.

INTERESTING FACT

Jenner inoculated his 11-month-old son with the cowpox virus to test his theory.

Carl Linnaeus

Carl Linnaeus was a Swedish naturalist, botanist, and zoologist. He classified various plant and animal species by naming them using the binomial system.

Childhood

Carl Linnaeus was born in Smaland, Sweden, on May 23, 1707. Carl developed a keen interest in flowers and plants at a young age. His father saw that he was interested and encouraged him by teaching him some fundamentals of botany. He gave him his plot of ground to grow plants on and explained the various names of various plants.

Education

He graduated from medical school in Holland and began practising medicine right away. In 1741, he started teaching botany at the University of Uppsala. He frequently went on plant-finding expeditions to remote locations like Lapland.

INTERESTING FACT

It is said that whenever Carl was upset, he was given a flower that instantly calmed him down.

Binomial Nomenclature

Carl Linnaeus' most important contribution was binomial nomenclature. First, he classified plants based on the number of floral parts they had, such as stamens and pistils. Then he devised a system in which plant and animal names consisted of a genus part and a species name, such as Homo sapiens. Based on his observations, he wrote several books, including *Genera Plantarum* and *Critica Botanica*.

John Dalton

John Dalton was an English chemist who established modern chemistry. His study of colour blindness turned out to be a boon for those who are unable to distinguish one colour from another.

His Life and Education

John Dalton was born in 1766 in England to a weaver family. John learned mathematics, Latin, and Greek with the help of his blind and gifted colleague, John Gough, by teaching other students during his teaching years. Later, in 1793, he was appointed as a mathematics professor at New College in Manchester, where he conducted various studies. Later, he gave private tutions and worked on numerous books and experiments until he died in Manchester in 1844.

Dalton's atomic theory

Dalton asserted that the loss of colour in the eye's liquid medium is what causes colour blindness. Following his research on colour blindness, Dalton developed his most profound theory, the atomic theory, which stated that any given element was made up of the same atoms of similar mass. Furthermore, all elements have different properties because they are made up of different mass atoms.

INTERESTING FACT

John Dalton used homemade instruments to keep a daily log of the temperature, pressure, and other weather conditions.

Charles Darwin

Charles Darwin was a British scientist who developed the theory of evolution and described the process of natural selection. His most famous book, On the Origin of Species, catapulted him to fame overnight.

Early life

Charles Robert Darwin was born on February 12, 1809, in Shrewsbury, England. He was made to enrol at Christ College, Cambridge, to become a parson. However, he was more interested in collecting plants, insects, and geological specimens with his cousin, entomologist William Darwin.

Life changing expedition

At the age of 22, Charles Darwin embarked on a five-year scientific expedition aboard the Beagle, sailing through Brazil, Argentina, and Chile. He then returned to England in 1836 and began studying the specimens he brought back from his journey. Charles Darwin published his evolution theory in his book *On the Origin of Species* in 1859.

Charles Darwin's Theory of Evolution

Natural selection served as the foundation for Darwin's theory of evolution. He described the process by which parents impart their best traits to their children. He continued by saying that when taken together, these traits created a new person that was distinct from their ancestors.

INTERESTING FACT

According to Darwin's theory of evolution, the Earth was formed 4.6 billion years ago.

Louis Pasteur

Louis Pasteur was a world-renowned French biologist and chemist. He is regarded as one of the most influential scientists, having discovered that germs cause the majority of infectious diseases. Pasteur also discovered vaccines for a variety of infections.

Childhood

Pasteur was born on December 27, 1822, in Dole, France. Pasteur had wanted to be a chemist since he was a child. When one of his friends was bitten by a wolf and infected with rabies, it left a lasting impression on young Louis. He resolved to learn more about the disease and find a cure for it.

Pasteur's Contributions

Louis Pasteur conducted experiments on molecular structure, which gave rise to stereochemistry, a branch of chemistry. Pasteur also developed the germ theory of disease. To find a solution, he developed several vaccines, including anthrax and chicken cholera vaccines. Later, he discovered a vaccine for rabies, a contagious infection caused by a virus that attacks the nervous system.

INTERESTING FACT

Joseph Meister, Pasteur's first rabies patient, worked as a caretaker at the Pasteur Institute.

Education

Pasteur discovered the pasteurisation process during his research in the University of Lille. It is the process of sterilising food by boiling it at a specific temperature. He saved France's beer, silk, and wine industries.

Dmitri Mendeleev

Dmitri Ivanovich created the Periodic Table, which is the most fundamental classification of matter's building blocks. A general chemistry professor at the University of St. Petersburg came up with a system for categorising the then-known elements based on their atomic weights and typical characteristics.

His life and Education

Mendeleev was born in Tobolsk, Siberia, on February 8, 1834. He joined the University of Heidelberg, where he conducted chemistry research and met many famous chemists of the time. Mendeleev returned to St. Petersburg in 1863 and began teaching chemistry, eventually becoming a professor of general chemistry at St. Petersburg University. During his lectureship, he wrote a textbook, Principles of Chemistry, and in 1869, he created the periodic table.

Mendeleev Periodic Table

Mendeleev's most important invention was the periodic table. He also predicted the properties of some previously undiscovered elements and left space in the table for them. After many years of research, he discovered three elements: gallium, scandium, and germanium. Mendelevium is the atomic number 101 element which is named after Dmitri Mendeleev.

INTERESTING FACT

In 1887, Mendeleev made a solo ascent in a hot air balloon as part of his interest in aeronautics.

Alexander Graham Bell

Alexander Graham Bell was a well-known scientist and inventor. His invention of the telephone ushered in a new era of communication technology. He rose to prominence as one of the world's most influential scientists.

His Life and Education

Alexander Graham Bell was born in Edinburgh, Scotland, on March 3, 1847. When he was 16, he began learning and researching speech techniques. In 1870, he relocated to Boston to teach at Sarah Fuller's deaf school. He also tutored private students; among them was Hellen Keller. In 1873, he was appointed professor of vocal physiology at Boston University and he ended up marrying one of his pupils, Mabel.

INTERESTING FACT

Alexander Graham Bell's mother was deaf, which motivated him to work on various speech systems.

Other inventions

After conducting a detailed research, Bell also discovered a machine called photophone which passes the sound with the use of light. He worked on inventions in the areas of aviation and hydrofoil boats.

His Telephonic Inventions

Alexander Graham Bell worked on how a human voice could be transmitted using a transmitter. In 1875, he invented the telephone, for which he received a patent in 1876. In 1884, the Bell Company built the first long-distance line, connecting Boston and New York. Bell also discovered a machine called a photophone, which uses light to transmit sound. He also worked on inventions for aviation and hydrofoil boats.

Marie Curie

Marie Curie was the most famous female scientist. She was the first woman to receive two Nobel Prizes. Her inventions in physics and chemistry made her famous all over the world.

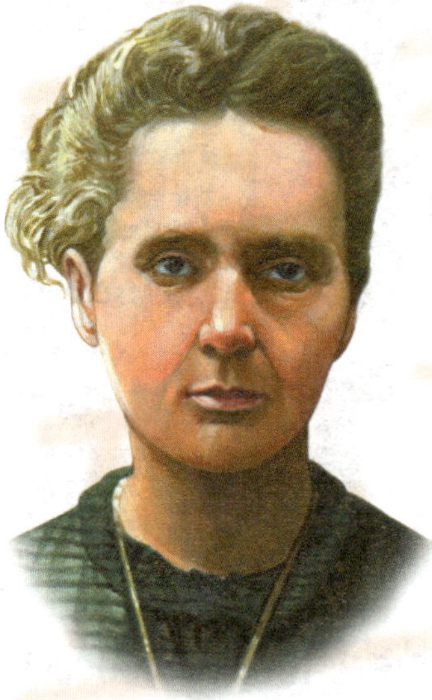

INTERESTING FACT

Element 96, Curium, was named in Marie Curie's honour.

Her Life

Marie Curie was born Marie Sklodowska on November 7, 1867, in Warsaw, Poland. She was denied admission to any Russian or Polish universities due to her gender and financial constraints. She became a private tutor and also worked as a governess to fund her higher education. She then moved to Paris to study physics and chemistry at the Sorbonne University. Marie soon became a teacher and met Pierre Curie, a physics professor.

Marie Curie, a Noble Laureate

Marie and Pierre Curie discovered that uranium ore contained components that were more radioactive than uranium after working together for many years in a leaky wooden shed. This uranium ore component contained two novel chemical elements. These two substances were given the names Polonium and Radium. She and her husband shared the 1903 Nobel Prize in Physics for this discovery. She won her second Nobel Prize in Chemistry in 1911 for the successful separation of pure radium.

Thomas Alva Edison

Thomas Alva Edison, one of the most well-known inventors of all time, is best known for inventing the incandescent lamp, also known as the electric bulb. Edison was an American inventor and scientist who created numerous imitations in a variety of scientific fields. He was one of the first scientists to imitate industrial research and teamwork in the invention process.

INTERESTING FACT

Thomas Alva Edison is credited with 1093 Patents.

His Life and Education

Thomas Alva Edison was born in Milan, Ohio, on February 11, 1847. When Thomas was seven years old, his family relocated to Port Huron, Michigan. He had no formal education and had only been to school for a few months. His mother taught him at home after he dropped out of school. He began working as a train boy at the age of 12 and sold newspapers and candy. He learned telegraphy from a station official while working at the station. This aided him in his work as a telegrapher. In 1869, he moved to New York to work as a full-time inventor.

His inventions

Thomas Alva Edison spent years trying to better the process of printing the telegraph. He created an electric pen in 1875, and in 1877 he created the phonograph. Soon after, he began researching Sir Joseph Swan's electric lightbulb. In 1880, his sustained efforts led to the creation of a 16-watt bulb. In addition, he created the Kinetoscope, a tool for watching moving pictures.

Albert Einstein

Albert Einstein, known as the "father of modern physics," was one of the greatest scientists ever. Even though Einstein was born in Germany, he acquired American citizenship in 1940. He published more than 300 scientific papers during his lifetime, and he introduced some of the most ground-breaking theories.

His Life and Education

Albert Einstein was born on March 14, 1879, in Wurttemberg, Germany, to a Jewish family. He was a genius from childhood, learning calculus at the age of 12. He studied at Aarau in Switzerland and was trained as a physics and mathematics teacher in Zurich. He was unable to find work as a teacher and instead worked for the Swiss Patent Office. He spent a lot of time there working on his research and writing several scientific papers. Einstein also formed a small discussion group with his friends to discuss science and philosophy.

Scientific Career

Einstein's scientific career took off when his paper on the capillary forces of straw was published in one of the leading science journals in 1901. In 1906, he was awarded a PhD by the University of Zurich, and that same year, he published four more papers that brought him widespread attention. One of these papers was on the photoelectric effect, for which he received the Nobel Prize in Physics later in life. Einstein's most ground-breaking work, however, was on the special theory of relativity, which had a significant impact on the understanding of various fields of science.

INTERESTING FACT

Albert Einstein was considered a slow learner due to dyslexia, a learning disability.

Alexander Fleming

Sir Alexander Fleming was an internationally renowned bacteriologist and pharmacologist. By discovering the first antibiotic, he etched his name into scientific history. Penicillin relieved the suffering of many people suffering from various bacterial diseases.

Life and Education

Alexander Fleming was born in Ayrshire, Scotland, on August 6, 1881. He graduated from medical school in 1906 and began his research in vaccines and immunology at the same institution. In 1908, he received a gold medal for being the best medical student at London University. He later worked as a lecturer and professor of bacteriology at St. Mary's School, where he published numerous works on immunology and bacteriology.

Discovery of Penicillin

Fleming discovered an enzyme called Lysozyme in tears and saliva during his research on tissues and secretions in 1921. He discovered mould while researching influenza in 1928. The mould grew on its own around the dish plates used to grow staphylococci germ, a germ that causes minor diseases. Fleming discovered that the mould formed a bacteria-free ring around itself after experimenting. Further research on the mould enabled Fleming to discover penicillin, which was later developed for use as a drug.

INTERESTING FACT

During World War I, Fleming also worked in battlefield hospitals in France as a captain of the Army Medical Corps.

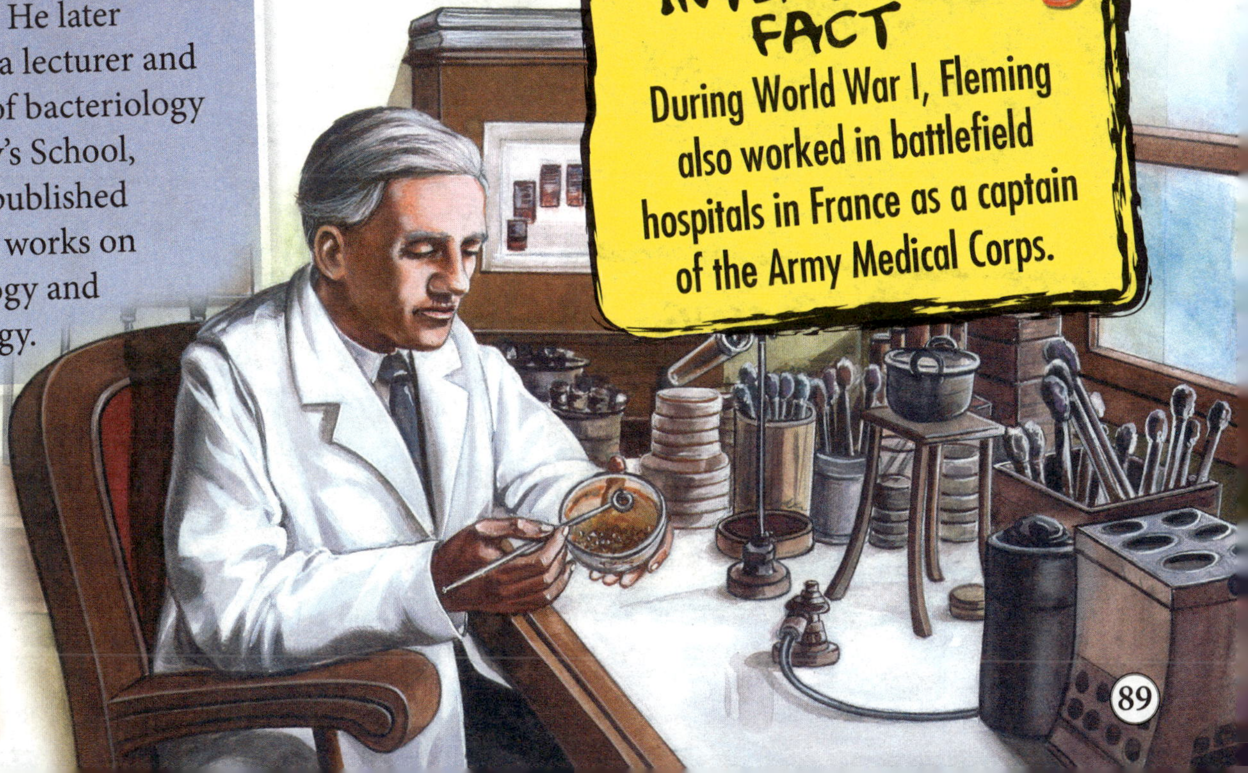

Edwin Hubble

Edwin Powell Hubble was an astronomer who is regarded as one of the world's foremost cosmologists. Hubble discovered the expansion of the universe and established Hubble's law. He demonstrated his point by learning about galaxies other than the Milky Way.

Early life and education

Edwin Powell Hubble was born on November 20, 1889, in Missouri, USA. In 1910, he graduated from the University of Chicago with degrees in mathematics, philosophy, and astronomy. Hubble went to work at Yerkes Observatory in Wisconsin to study astronomical theories. After finishing his doctorate in 1917, he served as an army major in World War I before joining Mount Wilson Observatory in California.

Contributions

While at Mount Wilson Observatory, Hubble studied the universe with the Hooker telescope. He discovered several spiral nebulae that he concluded were too far away to be part of the Milky Way. However, Hubble's observations revealed that there were other galaxies in the universe apart from the Milky Way. Hubble also discovered that all of these galaxies were moving away from each other at a consistent rate.

INTERESTING FACT

NASA, the American space agency, named the Hubble Space Telescope after Edwin Hubble.

Jane Goodall

Jane Goodall is a well-known primatologist (someone who studies animals like apes and monkeys) from the United Kingdom. Her well-known studies of chimpanzees gave other scientists a new understanding of the species and thus, established her reputation.

Childhood

Jane Goodall was born on April 3, 1934, in London, England. She was fascinated by animal behaviour from a young age and enjoyed spending time outside with animals. She once sat inside a hen house for hours, to observe how hens lay eggs. She worked as a secretary after finishing her schooling at the age of 18 to save money for her dream trip to Africa.

A chimpanzee specialist

Jane Goodall spent many years living among the wild chimps at Gombe Stream Chimpanzee Reserve. During her studies, she wrote an article about chimps called My Life Among Wild Chimpanzees. Jane provided a detailed analysis of the relationship between creatures and their surroundings, and what influences their behaviour, in her writings. In 1965, she received her doctorate in ethology from Cambridge. She also established the Jane Goodall Institute for chimpanzee conservation.

Trip to Africa

When Jane was 23 years old, she travelled to Kenya where she met Dr Louis S.B. Leakey, a palaeoanthropologist. He gave Jane the responsibility of researching chimpanzees and other primate behaviour. This meeting ended up being the beginning of Jane's research on chimpanzees.

INTERESTING FACT

Jane Goodall still has the chimpanzee toy that her father gave her when she was a young child.

Stephen Hawking

Stephen William Hawking was a great English physicist and cosmologist. He studied theories such as the big bang and black holes to learn more about the universe's life and nature. He also contributed to a number of books, including one of his best-selling titles, A Brief History of Time.

Early life

Stephen William Hawking was born on January 8, 1942, in Oxford, England. His father was a well-known medical researcher who encouraged his son to pursue a career in medicine. Stephen, on the other hand, chose physics and mathematics. After receiving his B.A. in Physics from Oxford University, he went on to Trinity College to pursue his PhD in cosmology.

Hawking's Contributions

Stephen Hawking studied the laws that govern the entire universe. He proposed the theory of singularity, which states that everything was densely gathered at one point. After billions of years, that dense body exploded, resulting in the creation of time and the universe. He uncovered evidence to support the big bang theory of the universe's origin. He concluded that black holes, a region of space, are not completely black and emit radiation.

Life after illness

Stephen Hawking was diagnosed with Lou Gehrig's disease when he was 21 years old, which caused the nerves that controlled his muscles to shut down. He became a well-known figure in the world of science after completing his doctorate in 1966 and conducting extensive research on black holes. Stephen received numerous medals and prizes, including a membership to the United States National Academy of Sciences.

INTERESTING FACT

Despite his disease motor neuron, Hawking continued his research and made several discoveries.

Glossary

Aeronautics: the science or practice of building or flying aircraft.

Amplitude: the maximum extent of a vibration

Apprentice: a person who is learning a trade from a skilled employer

Botanist: an expert in the scientific study of plants.

Chemist: a person engaged in chemical research

Colour blind: unable to distinguish certain colours

Conquer: take control of someone or something

Degree: an academic rank given by a college or university after examination

Discover: to find something during a search

Dyslexia: a learning disability that affects reading

Eliminate: completely remove or get rid of

Entomologist: the study of how insects relate to their environment

Experiment: a scientific procedure done to make a discovery

Honour: regard with great respect

Immune: totally or partially resistant to a particular disease

Immunology: the study of the immune system

Improve: to make something better

Influential: having a great impact on someone or something

Instruments: a tool

Invention: the act of creating something

Labour: make great effort

Matter: physical substance in the universe

Mentor: a trusted adviser

Mould: a furry growth of minute fungi

Naturalist: a person who studies plants, animals, and other living things

Parson: a member of the clergy

Pasteurisation: the partial sterilisation of a product

Philosopher: a person learned in philosophy

Pistils: the female organs of a flower

Principle: a general truth on which other things can be based

Revolve: to move in a circle on a central axis

Rotate: to move in a circle around a centre

Significant: to be worthy of attention

Species: a kind or sort of someone or something

Stamens: the male organs of a flower

Stereochemistry: the study of the arrangement of atoms in molecules

Sterilise: to make something free from bacteria

Zoologist: an expert of the behaviour of animals

Notes